'Smilin with my I

A novella by

Lasco Atkins

Published by New Generation Publishing in 2015

Copyright © Lasco Atkins 2015

First Edition

The author asserts the moral right under the Copyright, Designs and Patents Act 1988 to be identified as the author of this work.

All Rights reserved. No part of this publication may be reproduced, stored in a retrieval system or transmitted, in any form or by any means without the prior consent of the author, nor be otherwise circulated in any form of binding or cover other than that which it is published and without a similar condition being imposed on the subsequent purchaser.

www.newgeneration-publishing.com

New Generation Publishing

Dedicated to Miranda

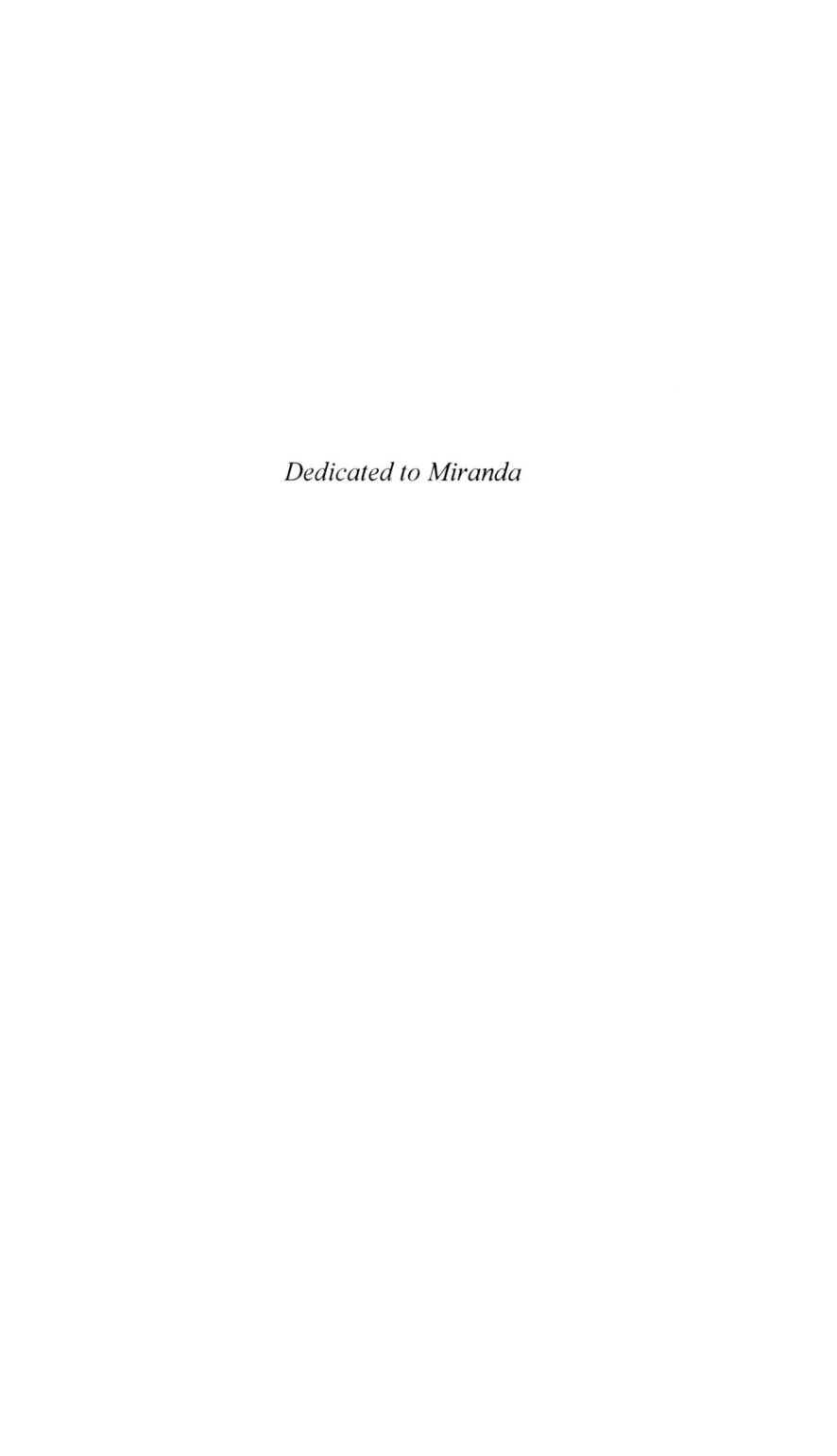

CHAPTERS

Foreword i
CHAPTER 0 – INTRO 1
CHAPTER 1 - ARRIVALS 2
CHAPTER 2 - LONDON 6
CHAPTER 3 - DAM.. 15
CHAPTER 4 - RETURN 30
CHAPTER 5 - ARIZONA 37
CHAPTER 6 - DAMNED.. 40
CHAPTER 7 - NOWHERE 47
CHAPTER 8 - THE TRIP ..……………………….... 58
CHAPTER 9 – BACK AGAIN 70
CHAPTER 10 – COPS 76
CHAPTER 11 – AFTERMATH 84
CHAPTER 12 – FINALE 87
AFTERWORD.. 90
ENERGY 92
TRIPPING IN FILMS... 97
TRIPPING IN TV 106
TRIPPY FILMS ……………………………..…..108
ACKNOWLEDGEMENTS 114

Foreword

Many people are put off by cannabis and magic mushrooms. This tale is of the light and dark side of the drugs. I have personally had the best and worst times on drugs. They have changed me on a spiritual level and definitely affected my whole outlook on life. When I was younger I wanted to 'trip' forever feeling the eternity of the spiritual drug. However, at the back of my mind I always had questions about dreams and death. As I got older I stopped taking hallucinogens completely since two of my main questions were answered. When I finally got the answers on 'the other side' it wasn't quite what I expected. The first few times were fun, but then they became deadly serious and I realised it was no longer a joke. Many people suffer from mental issues, even I've had a mild depression as a young teenager. In a way weed and shrooms sorted me out and gave me a new outlook on the world after every experience.

Nowadays I miss the good times, but the bad times definitely made me stop. Experimenting with Class A pharmaceuticals is an easy substitute, but part of me is jealous of people my age that still trip let alone old hippie couples at festivals. I feel like I've aged quicker than most of my peers. In spiritual years I have surpassed 100's of aeons yet still certain drugs like DMT (death-rebirth), share the similar experience that I feel like I have already been there in a way.

This story is my most personal since many of the occurrences happened to me for real. Fictional experiences including the family ties are there for emotional reasons purely making this a drama more than what my life was. We did move around a lot as children so were always subjugated to different social circles and cultures, this has expanded my knowledge of the world and the planet. Drugs in various countries (including Peyote in Mexico) and environments lead to a unique perception of the places and the people. Tripping is like going to the gym: it is very personal and impersonal at the same time. By this I mean you can have mates there but in the end, the experience is down to you.

CHAPTER 0 – INTRO

I sit on a large beach in California at dawn. No one is there except for me. *Ashes to Ashes* by Faith no More is playing on my MP3 player. I'm sitting alone on the beach engulfed in emotions of my memories. Waves are splashing on the seashore; sounds of seagulls are heard as they fly high above and around my head. My long hair flows loosely in the early morning breeze, my ponytail is undone. Remnants of my dreadlocks remain, now less tangled than once a long time ago. I speak to you as I reminisce, my name is Lorraine, but you can call me Lo for short.

Since you hardly know me let me start at the beginning of my inner spiritual journey. You'll get me pretty quick. I arrived in London after being constantly moved around the world time and time again. I was visiting with my brother J, who I haven't seen in ten years, but there were . . . . complications let's say, I'll explain . . .

CHAPTER 1 - ARRIVALS

I arrive at Heathrow airport outside London Terminal 5. I have on my usual baggy clothes and semi-dreadlocks for hair. I'm listening to Radiohead (Paranoid Android) on my MP3 player as I come out of arrivals; J is already waiting for me. J is also dressed in baggy clothes, but being the older brother he is still taller than me. I guess I've always been a tomboy as long as I can remember; maybe I just dug guys' style more. I pull my headphones out. He has a sign with "dumb ass" written on it. I see this and immediately start to crack up (laughing). I go over to him and throw my arms around him and we hug tightly. We both have American accents, from international schools. He has kept his despite living here for ten years. J notices my dreads but does not say anything, accepting that his sister has changed in the past ten years. We had grown apart once he went to boarding school then college over here. We used to be close as kids, but that's why I'm here telling you this story. I wanted to connect with him again, like when we were younger, accept now we are both adults.

J blurts, 'damn yo you have grown!'

I reply, 'look who's talking, I haven't seen you in what?'

'Ten years.'

'Ten fuckin years man!'

J offers, 'damn! Here let me grab your bag.'

J chucks his sign in the bin and we walk off together heading for the carpark, every now and then we punch each other in the arm and chuckle. I'm crying slightly, wiping my tears away, hiding it from my brother. He takes sneaky peeks at my hairdo.

It wasn't always like this. We just hadn't seen each other for years you know. We used to get into fights all the time, but which siblings don't right? Once he got sent to boarding school, we lost that special bond siblings have.

He changed, like someone in prison you know? He wasn't as happy when he would come visit us back home (in the US). When he was around he was just trying to get fucked up anyway he could; steal our folks' booze, whatever. Even I remember getting proper wasted with him the first few times. He grew up way too fast for his own good, and I got stuck with our parents. I was supposed to go to the boarding hell hole too, but my brother got into loads of trouble and was nearly expelled. So our Mom threatened to divorce Dad if I ever got sent. It all worked out in the end, he got to come home, and Arizona was where home was at the time. That was a pretty sweet time for all us. Despite the fact Mom was going off the rails drinking; guess where my bro got the genes from? Oh did I forget to mention he had brain surgery? Yeah he could've been a veggie, but came out all good.

J is driving as I look out of the window. A cool music track by *Thievery Corporation* is playing on his stereo. I try to take in the view as we drive from the airport (Heathrow) to partial countryside to inner London. We talk most of the journey, but don't keep eye contact the whole time. It is my first time in the UK; I'm not used to fish & chips, and London traffic! It is drizzling too now BTW.

J breaks the silence, 'so watcha been up to the past few years? I sort of lost contact with you guys, I'm not even sure where you even were.'

I reply with, 'dis and dat, you know. I finished my Art College degree then kinda bummed around for a bit saving up some cash to come visit here. I just had an exhibition, shame you couldn't make it.'

'I know, I'm real sorry, but as you'll soon find out London is expensive and I couldn't even afford to come visit anymore. I'll make it up to ya, I swear.'

'It's all good, we all been kinda busy. The folks say hi.'

J ignores this last comment, 'ah fuck em. What was your exhibition like?'

'You mean the location?' I ask slurring my words, still

jetlagged.

'Nah, your work, what did you exhibit again?'

'Ah, you mean my subject? Um, well, aliens.'

J laughs heartily, 'aliens huh. I suppose you always were the weird one, ha!' J rubs my head, and then grossed out wipes his hand on my arm jokingly.

I continue making small talk, 'well some of it was pretty cool anyway. I had all mixed media.'

'What's that? Mixed media?'

J never studied art; he went for a business degree but never finished it. J was a quitter a lot of the time whereas I was a finisher.

'Oh, it's like when you have different art forms. I had metal work, paintings, photography, all in the installation.' I explain.

'My little siss the artist, eh? Cool, did you bring any pictures with to show me?'

I smirk and rub my head, moving the dreads round to the back of my head and tying them into a ponytail. 'I think I just might if you behave that is.' Finishing off tying up my hair.

J grabs me in a headlock, as we swerve in the road. We both laugh as I wriggle my way out of it.

'I had the wickedest music playing too.'

J enquiries, 'like what, some trippy shit I hope.'

I confess, 'Umma Gumma and Spaces. You remember them right? Like all the cool music you would introduce me to first when you came and visited that is?'

J confirms with, 'killer, Pink Floyd and Grateful Dead, huh? You still listenin to that stuff?'

'You saying you don't anymore?' I ask curiously.

'Only when we're trippin yo.'

I'm sceptical of this last remark, 'fair enough, who's we?'

'Oh me and Kay, you'll meet her soon. She's my missus mate.' He says proudly in a cockney English accent.

'OK, you didn't tell me about-'

J cuts me off - 'she's cool, don't worry. She parties too.'

Excitedly I chip in, 'sweeeeeet, I can't wait to meet her. Also, by the way, at my exhibition I had black lights and a UFO hanging from the ceiling as if floating in space.'

J compliments his sister, 'cool yo. I wish I could've been there. Once you're here, you kinda get stuck, and can't leave anywhere financially unless your already made or upper class that is.'

Sceptically I ask, 'you gotta be exaggerating right?'

'I'm just kidding. It's an alright place all in all.'

'London isn't like I imagined it at all, bro.'

At that moment the rain starts to increase, as it gets cloudier above us. The song on the stereo changes to something slightly more depressing.

'Oh yeah and by the way it rains a lot . . . all the fuckin' time!'

I jokingly say, 'well I guess it's a change of scene alright.'

We both laugh heartily, as J accelerates away from the traffic lights. I see *god rays* as bits of sunlight shine through pockets in the clouds.

CHAPTER 2 - LONDON

J's apartment is in South west London, near Shepard's Bush and Hammersmith, a little place called Stamford Brook right by the tube station. His lounge is an average sized room with a main couch in front of the TV, a PlayStation 1, and a stereo connected to the TV.

'Mi casa, su casa,' which translates to *my house, your house* in Spanish.

'Gracias. Dude you got a PlayStation! Awesome.' They are huge in the States; Sony is king of the consoles in my mind.

J changes his tone. 'There is still a few other things you don't know about me too.'

'Nothing all too bad I hope.' I'm concerned for a moment.

J pulls out a bamboo and a coconut bong and shows them to me. Which to choose from? What a choice? I look both over then go with the coconut one. I have a big smile on my face, as he passes it to me. I take a lighter off a shelf and spark it. I immediately start coughing my lungs out.

J laughs.

I'm pissed, 'dude, you have fuckin tobacco in there?'

'That's how people smoke over here.'

Still coughing I manage a, 'grossssss. You know in the States we only smoke with pure yeah?'

'Sorry siss, I should've warned ya.'

I sarcastically reply, 'ya reckon?' My eyes go bright red and start to glaze over, as the tobacco hits me. I pass the bong back to J, who takes it and kills the rest of the hit. He coughs a little too, but not as hard as me. My tender virgin lungs have yet to understand the difference between smoking pure and not.

J apologises, 'it'll take some getting used to, but you'll be aight. You still smoke ciggies right?'

'Yeah, but I'm so used to smoking da herb pure, you know?'

'I gotcha, tell you what. If you buying, maybe we can get some weed or skunk later.' J trying to find a compromise.

'Why? What was that stuff?'

J confirms, 'tobacco wit hash baby. Hell yeah!'

'Hash, huh? Not bad, I suppose.'

'We call it soap round here, just in case anyone asks on da sly.'

I concur, 'soap. Got it. Check.'

J changes the subject. 'Enough reminiscing, let's hit the station, shall we? Tekken or Wipeout?'

'How bout both?'

'Sure, we gotta meet Kay at her bar later, but we got some time to kill I guess.'

We both go and sit down on the couch after J turns on the PlayStation and TV; he has the stereo connected so the sound is in stereo to boot. I smile again, stoned as. J takes a hit off a joint that is resting in the ashtray. He offers it to me, but I decline for now.

I chuckle, 'I'm still high as fuck man!'

J speaks out like an announcer, 'all good, game on.'

The next few hours we spend on playing video games, smoking and laughing.

Kay's Bar has cool music playing in the background. We arrive right on time as Kay finishes her shift behind the bar.

J enters first and holds his arms up. 'Welcome to my humble abode.'

Still stoned I ask, 'I thought your house is your humble abode?'

J answers, 'that's where I pass out. This is where I live.'

Kay comes round the side of the bar and greets them. Kay hugs and kisses J first, as I stand next to them and feeling like a third wheel. I watch them slightly shy with my head down. Since Kay is Dutch/Kiwi she is quite open and friendly, she turns to me and I hold out my hand expecting a handshake. She immediately gives me a hug too and kisses me on both my cheeks (European habit I guess). This makes me feel at ease right away, since in actual fact I'm a lesbian, so I always enjoy female attention. I grin once again still jetlagged yet content.

Kay starts the conversation with, 'before we go sit down shall I get us a couple drinks on the house?'

I perk up, 'sounds good to me.'

J pitches in his two cents, 'good thinking babe, I see a free table over there. Need a hand?'

Confidently Kay replies, 'nah, I'm alright. I do this for a living right?'

'OK, OK. See ya over der den.'

She walks off calling over her shoulder. 'Won't be a sec.'

J and I go over to the table and sit down. When I put my arms on the table it's all sticky. I'm kinda grossed out, but J warns me, 'watch out for spilled drinks, that'll be us later. Ha ha.'

I laugh awkwardly, still a little stoned from earlier. We had a couple bongs just before we left the apartment. That's when I spot a girl standing alone by the bar, who shyly looks toward me, we share a glance. A possible coupling?

Kay comes into view with three pints of lager, she plops them down on the table. She wipes sweat from her forehead glad her shift is over.

'So, Lorraine is it?' Kay picks up the conversation whilst sitting down next to me.

'Lo actually, nobody calls me my birth name any more.'

Kay knowing we will get along instantly replies, 'sweet as. I've heard some stories of when you and J were younger, but like him I don't know much about what you been doin recently.'

'J can fill you in, but mainly I just graduated from Art School.'

J finishes off my sentence, 'and she had an awesome

alien exhibition.'

I give him a stern look, to check that Kay is all cool with aliens.

Kay, bonding, 'cool, I love aliens.'

I sigh in relief.

Kay pulls out a pack of smokes and offers me one first then one to J. I take it reluctantly at first; J throws his into his mouth. He misses a couple times, but then gets it just before Kay lights it for him.

'I tried to quit before I left, but it's kinda hard when all your friends are chain smokers you know?' I take the lighter and spark my own cancer stick.

'I know that feelin sista. This is London, pretty much everyone smokes here. Even all the foreigners.'

I continue, 'it is a hard habit to break out of.'

'Cheers to that.'

Kay raises her glass for a toast, J and I join in. Kay carries on, 'here's to . . . Not quitting, ha!'

As if on the same wavelength J and I blurt out, 'fuck quitting!' We all laugh as us girls take a sip each, J downs his whole pint.

'Damn boy! Slow down.' Hoping I'm heard this time.

'I guess you haven't realized your brother has to do everything more in excess than everyone else.'

Understanding I say, 'it's startin' to come back to me, you're right.'

Kay chirpily replies, 'true dat!'

J stands up, and grabs his empty glass and turns towards them. 'I'm getting' another one. You guys want something?'

Kay and I look at each other's pints that are barely touched. I shake my head no, but Kay thinks for a moment. She leans in close to me. 'How about a shot then?'

'Yeah, OK sweet. Go on then.'

J is getting impatient, needing his fix. 'Shot of?'

Kay looks up sweetly at him, 'whatever you decide. I trust ya.'

He looks at me for confirmation; I nod in agreement and take another sip of my pint.

'Cool, three mystery shots coming up.'

J walks over to the bar, leaving *us girls* to chat alone.

Kay, enjoying the vibe and my style, 'so you got an American accent like your bro huh?'

'Yeah, it's from international schools, but I spent the last few years with my Mom. Dad left us years ago.'

'Sweet as. It's kinda weird that some people never seem to get rid of it. Huh?'

I'm enjoying where this conversation is going, 'did you go?'

She confirms my suspicions. 'Yeah, same as you guys. That's something we all have in common, eh?'

'Yeah, I guess, huh? What about you though, where you from? Where'd you grow up, etcetera?'

I take another sip from my pint as Kay lays down her family story, 'well my parents are Dutch and Kiwi. I grew up all over like you guys. NZ, Holland, Spain, and now here.'

'We had a spell in Indonesia, but I only ever visited New Zealand on one holiday.' As if bragging now.

Kay sips her lager again. 'I spent a few years there; they definitely got the best music scene in the world.'

'For real? What about here? I heard a couple cool bands that come from the UK.'

Kay enlightens her new best friend, 'ah, it's mostly pop crap. I'm not really into the radio music they play over here.'

I agree, 'I hear dat.'

J comes over with the shots and his new pint. We clink our shot glasses together and cheers. J slams his glass down on the table, and makes a loud howling noise. Kay and I laugh as we lean towards each other.

J stands up and puts on his English accent again, 'well ladies, if you'll excuse me I have some business to attend to.' J takes a little bow before he heads to the nearest fruit (gambling) machine. Kay is already used to this behaviour, but I'm slightly disappointed in my brother being a bit distant. I was hoping for quality time, but each to their own I guess.

Kay throws her arm around my shoulder consoling me with, 'don't worry about him, you know he's got that addictive personality thingy goin' on.'

'I know, I just never really got gambling. He must have that gene from our Dad.'

'Don't worry, he doesn't always lose, he wins most of the time.'

Kay licks out the rest of the shot glass, Sambuca I think.

I'm trying my hardest to sound interested. 'Well I could always give it a go, maybe later perhaps.'

Kay speaks in an American twang, 'girlfriend, you here to stay yo!'

As we continue talking, I keep exchanging looks with the girl at the bar. After a while, Kay excuses herself to go to the toilet. I sit there for a moment by myself before I decide to go talk to the stranger. I stand up a bit tipsy; wobble a bit due to the head rush from getting up so quick.

I boost my confidence saying out loud, 'wow head, rush. Come on girl.' The girl from the bar looks up happily, to see me advancing towards her. Then all of a sudden J wins the jackpot and starts cheering loudly nearby. I stop for a moment; he turns and spots me approaching the girl at the bar. J waves me over and I change course and head towards my bro and the fruit machine instead. He is making lots of noise, slightly embarrassing me. Then for some crazy reason I jump on top of J's back out of excitement. Kay comes out of the toilet behind them, and jumps on top of us. We lose our balance, and nearly tip over, but Kay jumps off in time to avoid this. I guess my chance with the *bar girl* have gone out the window. After J has calmed down a bit, we all sit back down at the table. He has a big smirk on his face, looking very pleased with himself. After a minute or so I look to the bar once more, but the girl is gone from her seat. I look around the room, but can't spot her anywhere, I sigh to myself.

Back at J & Kay's place later that night. Kay is asleep on one of the side chairs, as J and I are playing the console again. Tea Party's *Winter* track is playing on the stereo instead of the usual PlayStation noises. We are both slightly drunk still and also proper stoned too now.

I break the silence. 'Do you remember the sunset in Arizona?

J remembers the colours, 'can I ever forget it?'

I recall being on the porch as the sun is going down (magic hour), Mom watches on from behind the screen door. Is it a memory? Or my imagination?

J snaps me out of my mini fantasy. 'Heh, changing the subject. What you think about goin' to Amsterdam in a few weeks?'

'You mean the three of us?' Hoping Kay will be there too.

J explains, 'na, just you and me. Kay will probably have to work; she is a slave to the trade mostly.'

I think about it, 'sure, I'm down. I haven't been to Holland yet.'

J with red eyes tokes a joint then blows out a cloud of smoke towards the TV. 'All the bud you can smoke, and it's legal!'

I contribute to the subject, 'yeah, I heard somethin about that. They got those coffee shops, right?'

'That's the one. So? You in?'

I take the spliff from my bro, 'definitely. That means I get to smoke pure, huh?'

'Whatever you want siss. They got fresh shrooms too.'

I ponder for a moment; I only ever took Acid or LSD back home. Never organic trips, only chemical. 'You mean like psilocybin, the magic ones?'

'Fuck yeah; I've been a couple times. You can buy em in the coffee shops too, so we don't even have to leave all day long if we don't want.'

'Just smoke and trip, eh?'

J smiles broadly. 'Can you imagine a better life?'

'Shame we can't live there.' I actually consider this for a few beats.

'You wouldn't want to. You'd be a walking zombie. I know I would. I mean I've already been couple times. It's crazy.'

I remind him, 'that's right, Kay reminded me of your *do it more than anyone else* rule.'

'I wouldn't call it a rule; it's more a personal choice thing.'

I'm concerned now, remembering the drama back in the day, 'is it all OK with your brain surgery, do you still have any side effects?'

'That's all in the past, think about the future Lo. Give us a chance to catch up spiritually.'

I think of the past as I speak, 'shit. When was the last time we tripped together?'

'A long time ago, that's fo sure.'

I lay down some ground rules, 'alright, as long as we don't overdo it too much, and we keep an eye and ear open for each other. Yeah? Deal?'

J leans over and shakes on it. 'Deal.'

We both chuckle in excitement, thinking of the infinite possibilities we could experience.

Then Kay starts stirring in her sleep, and wakes up rubbing her eyes. There is still a heavy cloud of smoke hovering in the room. She waves her hand around, since she doesn't smoke weed, only ciggies. Kay had a bad experience when she was younger; she got really paranoid and even partially schizo so she never smoked it ever again. Kay sitting up now finds a cigarette and sparks it, 'what you stoners talking about? I heard something about a deal.'

I tell her, 'we just made plans to go to Amsterdam soon. In a couple weeks, maybe.'

'Well you can count me out, I gotta work plus I don't

smoke that stuff anymore.'

J addresses the subject, 'she gets paranoid whenever she smokes.'

'Everyone gets paranoid at times; it's just your brain fuckin with ya that's all.' Even I've experienced getting paranoid while smoking time to time, mainly due to cops, but never off a trip before.

Kay stands up now about to get ready for bed. 'Well, enough about me. Just take care of her, alright?' She crosses her arms when J doesn't respond instantly. She clears her throat getting J to answer.

'Of course I will she's my blood. Well half anyways'

Kay puts her hands on her hips for a moment looking like a stern housewife, 'well, from now on she's my sister too OK? And likewise, you keep an eye on him too for me will you!' Kay stretches and yawns. She comes over to give me a night, time hug. She squeezes a little extra before she breaks away. 'I'm goin' to bed you two. So try not to corrupt each other all night long will you?'

'Good night (I pause) my new sister.'

Like a kid Kay says, 'nighty night.' She exits to go upstairs to their bedroom, which is in the attic.

Orbital's *White Fluffy Clouds* is playing on the stereo. My imagination keeps drifting off into visuals of perfectly formed clouds appearing on the TV. I fast forward two weeks and transition from the living room to landing in Holland.

CHAPTER 3 - DAM

J and I both exit the train around noon, and put on our rucksacks properly, since we both have them on one shoulder each. I guess we've been doing it so long it's sort of stuck in the *cool psyche* of society. We exit the station and enter the world of Dam. As we walk down the streets by the canal, we walk by a few coffee shops; I'm getting antsy and impatient for a smoke. J insists on that we check in to our hostel first, and then indulge.

I suggest, 'what about that one? We can just go in and have one joint.'

J takes the decisive tone, 'once we start we won't stop. And we'll be doin' a lot of sitting high off our asses, trust me.' He knows what he's talking about, he's the experienced one here not me.

I'm the tourist here, 'OK, whatever you say Mr Expert.'

J spots the hostel he had in mind staying in again, since it was fairly priced from his previous trips. 'There it is, we'll dump our bags and then I'll take you to the "cream of the crop" in Dam.'

I get a wave of excitement as we are closer to our goal after all the travelling. First we enter *The Doors* coffee shop, coincidentally the band is playing on the juke box. We approach the *bar* and browse through the *menu*. J goes for some Kush, I'm a bit nervous still so after stalling choose from the Super Skunk variety.

We find a table to sit at and are both toking away on a fat joint each. J has a spliff (with tobacco) and I finally have a pure one. We have temporarily *rented* a small plastic bong, which is on the table too amongst other things. They do that at certain coffee shops; they offer pre-rolls, paraphernalia and always have spare roaches on the tables. It's like a diner with its ketchup or sauces yet in this case smoke related.

I blow out a haze of smoke, 'ahhhhh, this is da shiznit dog!' I can taste the quality of bud once more.

J tilts his head back, 'what did I tell ya?'

I feel all proud. 'We did it bro, we fucking did it man. We're finally here.'

J takes a huge toke off the joint, puffing his cheeks out trying to hold in the whole hit, but then exhaling most of it.

I take out some cash from my wallet, and get up. 'I'm gonna get some more, this is too cool.'

'OK, but conserve your money, it goes pretty quick and don't forget we gotta smoke it all in the next couple days. We can't smuggle any back, they have check points.'

I stand there for a moment dazed from the smoke, and then I stumble over to the counter and look at the (skunk) menu again. I see they have hash cakes and pre-rolls. I order a hash cookie, then head back to the table and split it with J.

I'm munching and chatting, 'I saw they have pre-rolls as well, so if we get too stoned to roll we can always get one of dem.' I break off half of the cookie and offer it to my bro.

J enlightens me, 'nah, you don't want those, they always mix it with way too much tobacco to rip off the stupid tourists that can't roll their own.'

'For real, fuck there's that plan out the window then.'

J plans ahead, 'don't worry I can still skin up when I'm fucked. Tell you what; we should get some mushies soon.'

'You mean da shrooms? Shouldn't we wait till nightfall?'

J slightly pissed, 'what da fuck for? We gotta make the most of our time. Am I right or am I right?'

'You're right brother-man.'

'Alright then, let's blow this joint.' Chuckling to himself. 'Get it.'

I take a moment then laugh out loud, covering my mouth thinking it was louder than it was. I take the last hits of my joint and stub it out in the ashtray. We gather our coats, bags of weed, and papers then leave.

We enter the Bulldog cafe on the main square in central Dam. J and I approach the counter, asking the (Dutch) *bartender*. 'Say, you guys got any shrooms?' J asks

The bartender seems like a cool guy, very knowledgeable on the subject. He has a techno look about him, shaved head with a mini coloured Mohawk he also wears jeans with suspenders with a white T-shirt, resembling a punk from the 80's. 'Ah, you like da magic ones, yes? Well, I have powder for de tee, and also we have da fresh ones.'

I can't believe what I just heard, 'fresh, eh? Cool, you mean for cooking right?'

The bartender laughs, and opens a fridge-like compartment drawer by his legs under the counter. He pulls out two big bags; then lays them on the counter. 'Dis ones, you can cook if you like, but some people just eat dem like dis.' He motions the ancient symbol of eating food with his hands.

J enquires further, 'and they two different types yeah?'

'Ja, dis one is Mexican, nice buzz but not as big as da Thai.'

I ask curiously, 'which ones are more popular, what would you recommend?'

The bartender responds with, 'if you like mild trip, I can make tea for you, yes. But if you are hard core you take da Thai.'

'Let me just discuss this with my business partner, cool?' J turns to me and leans in close like we're discussing a national secret or something.

'Sure ting, no problem.' The bartender notices and sees to a couple down the bar, they are Dutch and just want to have a drink for their date. They look at J and me like the tourists that we are, their eyes flick to the shrooms on the bar counter.

J discusses options, 'so what you reckon?'

'Well I heard Mexican are pretty good. Is it cool if we

try the Thai ones?'

J snorts, 'I don't give a shit, trippin is trippin right.'

'Sure. But as long as it's a spiritual trip,' I suggest. My journey here was to expand my mind, tap into my mind's eye or some shit. My bro on the other hand just wanted to get fucked up ASAP.

'We can make it whatever we want it to be. We are masters of our own destiny, right?'

Jokingly I reply, 'God, you're such a bad influence.'

J doesn't find this comment amusing, 'look who's talking. So we gonna do this or what?'

The bartender comes over after serving the Dutch couple. 'So all good ja? Which ones you go for?'

J makes his decision, 'we'll go for the Thai my man.'

'Good choice. If you need anything else, my name is Thys.' He sticks out his hand, J and I do *gangsta handshakes* with him. I giggle about the randomness of ordering shrooms over the counter. The bartender takes the Mexican bag and puts it back in the fridge compartment. J and I order a couple of cokes, pay for it all together, and then find a spot in a corner to sit.

Two Irish guys come into the bar, buy some bud then sit down next to us. They are quite chatty and offer us a hit off of a bong procured from the bar.

We are quiet temporarily since we feel our space has been briefly invaded.

Liam is a bit *twitchy* and the more talkative one, and tries to start a conversation. 'Wow, this is fuckin' great man. I love it over here, legal smoke an all. Not like back home. Fuckin hell, so where's you two from?'

J speaks up, 'London mate.'

Liam replies, 'right, Londoners is it? I'm from Dublin me-self like. At least we all from the UK, eh?'

Liam's friend is quietly toking the bong, as Liam is speeding his head off. They probably took some pills or something earlier.

'I hear an American accent, you yanks are ya?'

J corrects him, 'sorry to disappoint, we just world travellers yo.'

'Fair enough, but you here for the smoke yeah?'

J continues, 'oh you know, a bit of this a bit of that.'

'Fuckin too right mate. We just got some speed off some geezer on the street, you keen?' He offers us some of his foil wrap holding his hand out. His mate is nervous.

'Nah, not really right now. We're on a slightly different vibe.'

After J says that, I lean in towards him and whisper in his ear. 'You comin up yet? I might be feeling something already.' Just then, as I say it both of us start to *come up*.

J ponders, 'now that you mention it, I think it just started to hit me.'

'You seeing tracers or anything yet?' I ask.

'Just feeling slight euphoria, no visuals. What about you?'

I reply, 'I dunno, sort of. I mean I feel it too but no visuals either.'

At the next table, Liam and his buddy are whispering to each other giving us funny looks. They hurriedly finish their bong, and offer it to us.

Liam asks, 'say you two want to keep hold of the bong? Me and my mate gonna make a move.'

J slurs his words, 'we're all good, cheers though.' J starts to look off in the distance as if spacing out. Liam's mate smacks Liam's shoulder so they leave, dropping off the bong at the bar first.

I follow them with my eyes, and after they exit I focus my attention on some guys playing pool. I start to stare at their game, and then eventually I begin *staring one of them down*. I can't tell if he sees this at first so I think he's ignoring me. We keep making eye contact; it must be noticeable that we are tripping since J and I are acting strange. We laugh every now and as we smoke joints. We lean against each other in our seats as the two of us are *bonding spiritually* once again after years of being apart.

I try conversation again, 'Dude, it's so cool to see you again in this place. Damn, I love Holland man.'

'I know how you feel siss. Now you see why we can't stay here for more than a few days, we would lose it eventually.'

I frown and try not to think about the return journey, 'ah, don't talk about going back, not yet anyway. I'm having a better time now than I ever had on acid and LSD. I missed this, I missed -'

'- us. I know me too yo. It's great innit, I really feel like I'm, what's the word?

I finish his sentence for him, 'tripping?'

J's words come out distorted this time, 'yeah, that's it. Fuckin trippin man!'

I take another drag off the joint that was still resting in the ashtray, and out of the bottom corner of my vision I focus on the joint as the background goes out of focus. Peripheral movements begin in my vision. I see mild colour shifts and tweaking of the environment. At that moment we both have this overwhelming sensation of *coincidence*.

I ask, 'are you thinking what I'm thinking?'

We look at each other at the same time, and speak in unison finally along the same wavelength, 'that we've been here before.' We both freak out slightly at first, but then relax at the same time.

'Do you have the feeling this all could be a dream?'

J furthers the discussion, 'could be a dream or was a dream?'

I'm starting to grasp what I'm seeing and feeling, 'hang on, I swear this all of a sudden seems so familiar.'

'Same. Is that even possible?'

'Wait, this can't be. Can it?'

I'm starting to figure out what I'm sensing. That this exactly the same as a dream I had when I was younger. We look at each other and see the truth in each others eyes.

J remembers clearly now, 'me too, when I was younger. I've never really understood it until this moment.'

I can see where this is going, 'it's like I'm a kid all over again dreaming it once more. Dreaming it and living it at the same time. I didn't get it at first, but now it all makes sense.'

'This is a fuckin' revelation man.' J says loudly.

'It's not our brains tryin to fuck with us. I really believe this is happening right now. Every time I take a toke off the joint, I see the joint in the foreground and the background is blurry, you know?'

'I've got somethin like that, but I dunno if I can put it into words like that. Tripping is definitely connected to dreams.'

I'm getting deep now, 'connected to everything. Dreaming, us here right now, connected like you say. As if it's fate or destiny even.'

'I just had a thought. You know what? Were you in my dream too?'

Unsure I reply, 'I don't know, but I was totally here before in my dream I know that for sure.'

J explains himself, 'it's like I'm here one moment with you then I'm off in another universe, then back again.'

'In another world, cool bro. I'm like that too, but you know what this feels like a -'

We look at each other again, then together. '-de (pause) ja (pause) vu.'

This time we both laugh out loud, then cover our mouths since we get embarrassed for a moment forgetting that we're still sitting in a public coffee shop.

I lean in to my brother again, 'shhhhhh.' (Laughing quieter)

J is amazed that we figured this miracle out so quickly. 'That's it oh my god. Do you know what this means?'

I shrug and frown.

'That if this is a de-ja-vu, it means -'

'- that all de-ja-vu's are dreams we've all had as kids.'

'Hence the feeling of already experiencing this sensation before.'

J expands on this, 'if this is happening for us right now that means it's got to be the same for everyone. They just haven't tapped into that part of their brain yet.'

'It's like a secret of the world, and we've just uncovered it. I want to tell someone.'

J makes sure I understand my place, 'wait, let us come down first before we start babbling to people. Who knows maybe people might think were crazy and lock us up.'

We look around the coffee shop to see if anyone overheard us. There are only a few people about and no one seems to be paying attention to us at all. Still we lean in closer to each other yet again, this time I tap the side of my nose (an English practice I picked up).

'Good thinking. I'm with you brother. I've always been your little siss.' I'm comforted by his next comment.

'And I've always been your older brother, for whenever you needed me.'

'Man, it's so fucked up we haven't seen each other for like ever, and then we go to Holland and we open Pandora's box so to speak?'

J continues, 'you know, this has explained a lot of things for as long as I can remember.'

I agree, 'me too. I mean what we just discovered is that fate, destiny whatever you want to call it is for real.'

J takes a scientific approach, 'meaning that life is predetermined. And that we were meant to be here in this exact spot . . . tripping.'

'The subconscious is fucked up man. Dude, I hope this shit is the truth and we're not just off our heads.'

J is certain, 'I know this; I've never felt so sure of anything in my life before.'

'I know me too. I just still can't believe we never realized it without drugs. What should we do with this knowledge?'

'I say let's get some more shrooms and head back to the hostel.' Knowing he wants to get more fucked up seeing what the trip will tell us next.

I'm keen. 'Good idea, if we remember all this stuff tomorrow it's gotta be golden right?'

'Don't worry, we're not gonna forget this. Trust me.'

I come back with, 'I do trust you bro, we are family after all.'

J and I stand up and give each other a hug and shovel all our remaining drugs into our pockets. J goes over to the bar and gets some more shrooms as I look around to make sure we didn't leave anything. Still tripping, I stand up then I chuckle to myself that I'm slightly off-balance.

Fast forward to the hostel that night. J is lying on the bed opening and closing his eyes, while I sit at a small table concentrating on *skinning* up a joint. It's always a challenge when I'm tripping. J mastered the art years ago; I'm still a slight novice.

J sits up in his bed. 'You wanna watch some TV?'

'Sure let me just finish rolling first. It is always such a mission when I'm tripping.' I fumble with the paper, it keeps slipping out of my fingers and I'm slowly getting frustrated.

J sees this, stands up and comes over to the table, sits down and takes over *rolling duties*. 'Here, I'll do it, you check if there's anything good on TV.'

I stand up disappointed, but also happy to oblige since we haven't had a smoke for at least an hour. I start to space out in front of the TV, which is in the corner hanging above eye level. I flick through the channels on the TV, since there is no remote. I start to laugh in a crazy sort of way.

J looks up at me licking the gum on the Rizla paper.

I turn towards him. 'Dude, I still can't believe it. I think I'm still in that dream. No matter what channel I turn to, it's like I've seen them all before.'

J stands up sparking the joint, passes it to me and I step back to let my brother try the *TV test*. As he fiddles with the channels he has a similar sensation. 'It's like I dreamt it last night before we got here. It's so fresh in my mind it still seems like it happened just now.'

I toke on the joint as I speak. 'Exactly, this is still for real isn't it? I can't tell anymore, it just seems so weird.'

'This is doin' my head in let's just leave it on one channel and see what happens.'

I go back to my seat and mumble, 'good idea.' I pass J back the joint as he sits down at the table again. We watch the TV, but as we are both *coming down* we are getting a bit sleepy. We yawn from time to time. In the faint distance I start hearing night-time crickets like back home. I have a sensation my subconscious is by the desert. I don't mention it though, since I don't wanna put off J.

'I've got to tell you something J. I don't think I've told you before or if not for a long time, but I love you man.'

J smiles happily, 'I know siss. I know. Me too.'

I continue, 'I don't know if we'll ever connect again like we did today, but I just wanted to let you know in case I never say it again.'

J comes back with, 'or at least until the next time. Tripping I mean.'

'Not just the tripping, I mean us, life in general. I've never had so much fun before, honest.' I'm getting slightly emotional now, maybe it's the drugs.

'I don't wanna return to reality either, but it's inevitable.'

'Not if we stay here forever, you know?' I say hopefully.

'We're coming down now. You're just mumbling.' J being the realist all of a sudden.

'What I mean to say is, that I don't know if I can see people in the same light again. Be on their level, unaware of this great truth that's in all of us.'

J makes sure, 'except for me.'

'Except for you.'

We conclude the night, finishing the joint and lying down to sleep. I still hear the crickets as I lay my head on the pillow and feel like I'm back in Arizona in a way.

Remnants of Orbital's *Fluffy Clouds* song play in my head. The cricket noises fade as I drift to sleep. I dream of the desert and cacti with the clouds flying across the sky in time-lapse mode.

Groggy as, we both wake up around the same time, roughly around noon. Both of us still feeling dazed from the day before, get ready nice and slow as if in slow motion.

I begin the conversation, 'it's our last full day, what should we do?'

'How you feelin? Can you eat anything?'

'I dunno. All we had to eat yesterday was shrooms and that hash cookie.'

'Ha, we could try I guess, but my stomach is still fucked up from all that poison.' J rubs his belly, which in turn grumbles in return.

I scratch at my dreads, 'same, they tasted good though. Don't you think?'

J nods his head in agreement. 'I don't know why people are always so against the taste. They always gotta mix it with something, and end up puking anyway.'

'Pussies.' I chuckle.

'Maybe we should try splitting a burger or something, what you reckon?'

'OK, but you buyin' just in case I can't keep it down.'

'Now, who's the pussy?'

'Shut up. Whatever bro.'

I have taken a slight grumpy tone since I feel like I'm J's equal now; we did take the same amount of shrooms. Not that it's a competition or anything.

We split a burger from the nearest Burger King once outside.

Fast forward to sitting in another coffee shop. J and I are back at it, taking more shrooms this time a different type, having it as powder in tea. The caps float in the cups.

'You think it'll be anything like yesterday?'
'Dunno. We already uncovered one secret to the universe. Like my subconscious was asking the question, not me. You know?'
'I got no idea what to expect.' J is unsure of the future.

A couple hours pass into early night time. J and I are now walking around the streets of Amsterdam. *Mr Bungle* (Mike Patton's spin-off band) is playing in my head coming in and out as audible sound, sometimes muffled. We are stumbling through the red light district. Hookers are banging on the windows as we walk by, a black homeless guy is begging for money. J stops walking and is searching for change in his pockets, I wait impatiently ahead. This second trip it seems J is a bit more of a zombie and I have loads more energy than usual, my head is spinning.

'Come on J, fuck him. Let's go.'
J is still standing there tripping fumbling in his pockets. I go back and grab him by the sleeve. I mumble quickly more to myself, but J hears words here and there.

'Fucking niggas, always trying to rip us off.' I'm talking crazy since I'm not myself today; tripping two days in a row is taking its toll already. J is more peaceful and calm, but being too slow for my liking. Could I be going schizo?

'He just wanted some money for food.' J being chilled.

I'm mumbling quite a bit now, 'ya think? He fuckin' wanted it for drugs. That fuckin junkie! Damn kikes! World War two fuckers I know how Hitler felt!' I can't explain where this was coming from. I've never been a racist before but in the moment I was losing it, you could say.

J is getting genuinely concerned now; we've been tripping for hours now. 'Lo, what are you talking about? You're scaring me.'

I snap back at him - 'ah whatever, you pussy. I'm scaring you. What about yesterday? What we uncovered.

We're the gods (waving my arms around). They're just people. Maggots.'

'What's happened to you? You've changed.' J tries to grab my arm since I keep storming off bursting with crazy energy.

I shrug off his arm not liking physical contact in the headspace I'm in. 'Whatever bro, my eyes are open. This is my world now. We can't go back now.'

'Our ferry leaves tomorrow. What're you talking about? We have to leave.'

'Fine you go back, I'm not leaving. Fuckin niggas.'

J tries to reason with me, 'maybe we should go back to the hostel. This isn't right; this isn't the same buzz as yesterday.'

'Fuck yesterday! I'm living in the now.'

I stop walking so fast and turn towards my brother with a wild look in my eyes. I come across as quite aggressive as if I'm going to pick a fight. 'You are still my brother, right?'

J looks me directly in the eye, 'of course I am. Look, you're talking like an insane person.'

'Maybe I am, so what? What are you gonna do about it?' I see someone walk by, and follow him with my eyes. 'You feel like a fight. Come on let's go pick a fight. I'll take any fucker on right now!'

J suddenly grabs me by the shoulders and shakes me, I kind of snap out of it, but still I push my brother's arms off me and get in his face briefly. 'I thought you could handle this stuff maybe we should call it a day unless you calm the fuck down!'

I look down apologetically phasing out of my rage mode. He turns me around and we walk off quietly after that. I feel lonely and insecure. He was right.

Fast forward to the next morning in the hostel. J is *waking and baking* smoking a spliff occasionally looking at me with concern, recalling all of the previous day's events. I wake up to see him looking at me. 'You OK siss? I kinda lost you there for a while yesterday.'

I rub my eyes, 'shit, howd we get back? It went blank for a bit.'

'I got us back to the hostel, you we're talking and acting crazy. Do you remember any of it?'

'Bits and pieces. Fuck I'm burnt out as hell. How much did we take?' I can't recall if it was Thai or the Mexican that did me in.

J casually, 'oh just about seven times the normal dose.'

'Fuck, that's a lot. I don't think I've ever tripped that hard before.'

'Me neither. Two days in a row as well. We did more yesterday than our first day. We had to top the dosage cause of the tolerance in our system.'

I agree, 'yeah, and you always need more the second time around. We got any more money left?'

'Not really, we spent nearly all of it like maniacs! We should have let it be, I don't think we should have tripped yesterday.'

I disagree, 'ah whatever. Speak for yourself, if I recall it was you who said we should make the most of it while we're here.'

J is slightly worried when he hears me say *whatever* since it had a bad connotation the day before. 'All I'm saying is we had such a special first day, then yesterday you went a bit loopy.'

I reply with, 'did I? Well it's done now.' I turn over on my side away from my bro; he feels anxious but tries to continue the conversation anyway.

'You can't go back to sleep. We gotta get ready soon, or else we're gonna miss the ferry.'

'Ah whatever. Whatever bro.' I whisper then manage to nod off briefly. What feels like instantly, J wakes me up after his shower.

He shakes my bed covers. 'Come on Lo, we gotta go.'

I'm all groggy, roll over and back to my *normal* self. I am momentarily paranoid.

'Shit, what did I do? Did I do something bad?'

'No, it's all OK. Maybe you were possessed or something, you weren't quite yourself.'

Looking at my watch. 'Fuck me. We gotta go, we gotta hurry.'

'It's alright. Just grab your things. We'll make it, don't worry.'

We pack our things, have one last smoke, and as J waits in the hall I take one last look at our hostel room. Being spontaneous I say, 'good bye room. I'll miss all the good times we had.' I have a tear in my eye as I close the door.

CHAPTER 4 - RETURN

Back in London at King's Cross station. Kay is waiting for us at arrivals. She looks healthy and refreshed, whereas J and I look dishevelled. She is happy to see us and gives us both a hug at the same time, then a kiss on both of our cheeks. We walk down to the tube and chat the whole time.

'So what did you two devils get up to, eh?'

J and I look at each other sheepishly. I give him a look as if to keep our second day a secret from her.

'Oh you know the usual. Naughty behaviour.'

Kay looks us up and down, 'I bet. How you feeling Lo? You look like shit by the way.'

I acknowledge her comment. 'Thanks, I feel like I look. We had a wicked time though.'

She chirpily says, 'good, that's what I want to hear. Well, you're back in London now. No more legal weed for you guys.'

A look of concern is in Kay's eyes. 'You guys didn't smuggle anything did you?'

J and I double check our pockets, and then we give each other and her look to confirm we didn't. Even though we probably still stink of it.

'I don't think so. I hope not. We could have though we didn't get searched or anything.'

'Just remember what happened last time J.' Kay reminds him.

I ask curiously, 'why? What happened last time? You didn't tell me anything.'

J looks slightly embarrassed but chuckles anyway.

Kay enlightens me, 'last time we got back, J was super stoned still when we got off the ferry, and he got pulled aside by two MIB looking dudes.'

'They were dodgy as hell. I thought it was a hidden camera show or some shit.'

'Well what happened, for fucks sake?'

Kay answers, 'I had to wait outside the cop station for 2 hours while J was having a laugh being strip searched.'

My eyes widen. 'Noooooo!'

J continues the story, 'yeah, and while one searched me the other one just stood there in the corner looking like a statue or something.'

'So did you get busted or not?' Of course I'm curious how the tale ends.

'Hell no. Of course not. I didn't have anything on me. That's why I never smuggle anymore, ever since that fateful day. I was totally high and they knew it. But I had nothing on me so they had to let me go.'

'Right on, fuckin' lucky then.' I add.

Kay explains, 'luck had nothing to do with it. It was me that made sure he didn't bring any back. Remember honey.'

'Yeah, that's right. You made me give my last baggie away to some guy on the street. I ate some too.'

'Well wasn't that a nice thing to do. But Kay, I thought you said you don't smoke that stuff. What were you doing there the whole time?'

'I don't anymore, but I still do a bit of shrooms every once in a while.'

I find this a strange concept. 'You don't smoke but you trip. Cool, fair enough.'

We get on the tube, Kay snuggles up to J, and I chill on my own reading a movie magazine. I notice something out of my peripheral vision, distracted I look up from the film article. In total shock I see Islamic terrorists on the train with AK-47 machine guns and wearing balaclavas. They appear to come through the train and shout in Arabic. I look around the train; no one else can see this happen, only me. I stand up in an instant and kick the gun out of one of the terrorists' hands and grab the weapon. I then proceed to mow down all of them in one magazine. Smoke emulates from the barrel as I breathe heavily. A sweat bead appears on my forehead.

Then snap – I'm back in reality. Nothing has happened at all it was all in my mind. I wonder why this vision happened, or was it a flashback. I heard the urban legends way back when but never believed them until now. I just had my first one, I decide to keep it a secret and go back to my magazine as if nothing was wrong.

Fast forward a couple more days. J and I are sitting alone in his apartment; we've had a couple beers and a few bongs. The stereo is on playing some Tool, the *Aenima* album.

I start talking, 'you know I've got an open ticket to go back home.'

J takes this the wrong way, 'so why you tellin me?'

'Well, I can't decide if I should stay for the summer or go back home. I miss Arizona and Mom.'

'It's your decision. You make it.' He is unsure of my tone of voice.

I sit back in my seat, slightly depressed since J doesn't seem to be so passionate about his answers. As if he's giving me slight attitude.

'I was only asking to see what you thought.'

All of a sudden out of the corner of both our eyes there is an eerie black flash across the room. I go from slouching to sitting up immediately on the couch; we both look at each other for recognition that we both just witnessed it. We both get chills as if the temperature in the room just dropped momentarily. The hair on my arms and back of my neck stand up. Goosebumps litter my skin.

'Um. What the fuck was that?' I have fear in my voice.

'You saw it too?' J confers.

I try my luck talking to the room. 'Uhhhhh, OK. If there is a ghost in this room trying to tell us something? You know we don't mean you any harm, alright. But I'm assuming since we both saw something just now, you might be trying to tell us something. I couldn't have imagined it if you saw it too, right?'

'I definitely saw something. I don't have fuckin clue what that was, but it was some freaky shit that's for sure.'

I try and find an explanation, 'you don't think it has anything to do with our trip do you?'

'I have no idea; I've never seen anything like it before in my life. Was that a ghost or what?'

Just then the phone starts to ring, and we both jump off our seats briefly. Then afterwards we begin to laugh, in the process letting off some steam. J picks up the phone. 'She's here, I'll pass her over.' He hands me the phone, I take it reluctantly. I don't say much, but listen mostly. When I hang up I'm aware that I'm crying.

J asks aggressively, 'so what did she want?'

After a long pause. 'Dad just died. I have to leave tomorrow on the next flight back.'

'Well I guess you got your wish.'

J is being distant again focusing back on the TV screen.

Insulted I say, 'what? I didn't say I wanted to go back, I was just thinking about it. You wanna come? Mom would love to see you again.'

He replies, 'it's OK, you still have a parent. Mine were dead to me a long time ago, you know that.'

'Oh J, don't say that. It's not Dad's fault she slept with that random guy that one time. We still don't know all the facts bro.'

J adamant, 'I know enough. They both betrayed my trust by never telling me the truth. The divorce didn't make it any better either.'

I try my hand being the peacekeeper. 'Mom still loves you. You should come.'

'It's too late for that. I'm cool staying here.'

I fumble with the phone, 'I gotta call the airline now. I could always ask if they got any spare seats.'

'It's OK, you go on my behalf.' J is content in his position.

'We're still cool though, yeah?'

J confirms, 'yeah, we're still cool. So when you thinking of coming back?'

'I can't say right now, I guess I'll stay for the summer after all. Gotta make sure Mom will be alright. I'll give you a call after the funeral. Sweet?'

'Sweet as. Do what you gotta do. Fuck. You don't think that flash just now was him saying hello or good bye or something?

I contemplate, 'who knows. Is it OK if I crash on the floor in your room tonight? I'm not sure if I wanna be left alone in this room after that shit!'

J understands, 'sure. We can lay out some pillows on the floor. It'll beat the couch any day.'

'Cheers bro. Look, before I book my flight, can we do some special handshake or something. For us, so we know we'll be cool no matter what happens.'

J thinking about this one, 'what you thinkin?'

'I don't know; let's make a pact or something.'

'You mean like blood brothers?' J is unsure about this.

Enthusiastically, 'sure, since we're only really half related any ways.'

'You know I never really cared that we got different Dads.'

'I know. It was always how we felt about each other you know, like our trip to Dam. We soul twins brutha.'

J gets up. 'I get your point; I'll go get a knife. Ghosty or whatever you are you leave my sister alone, you hear me!' Pointing his finger around the room before he goes into the kitchen.

I chuckle at my brother's response. I look around the room, but it is dead quiet. Nothing.

J opens a drawer and pulls out his expensive sharp chopping knife. He comes back in the room and sits next to me, holding the knife in his hand.

'Wait, shouldn't we say something first?' I ask.

'Like what?'

'I dunno. How about your cool, I'm cool, together were

both -'

'- cool.' J finishes.

'Cheesy I know, but effective.'

'It's OK, for what it's worth I suppose.' J cuts a slit in his palm, and then I cut myself. We hold hands and let the blood mingle. It is like a moment from *Natural Born Killers* where Mickey and Mallory make the blood pact and the blood drips into a cartoon animation.

I speak first, 'cool?'

'Cool,' he adds.

'No matter what?'

J repeats, 'no matter what. Hug?'

After a second, we stand up and give each other a deep meaningful hug. I'm sobbing a little. J looks over my shoulder to see if the black flash is anywhere to be seen, but it never appears again. Likewise I check my side of the room. We split apart and I wipe my eyes a little, J places his arm on my shoulder. Then we sit back down, he hands me a tissue to wrap around my palm and he takes one for himself. It is not a deep cut so it's not like we're bleeding everywhere. He switches the CD in the stereo to Cypress Hill, *Hits from the Bong* begins playing. Once the intro has begun he packs a bong, handing it to me.

'I was thinking. I might be planning a trip to Holland again sometime. After the summer most likely maybe end of the year or something.'

'So soon? Yeah OK, who with?' I'm intrigued despite this really personal moment just now.

'Well the deal is Kay has got a family house in the country side. A couple hours outside of Dam.'

I take a hit from the bong. 'Sweet, tell me more.'

J continues, 'we could hit the coffee shops in Dam first, get supplies then hop on a train.'

'Sounds dope, when you reckon?'

'New years, siss.' He casually says.

'Fuck. New years? What a kick ass idea. Wait, hang on you mean for the Millennium?'

'Hell yeah! I gotta invite some of our mates, they been buggin me to get a trip together. New year's seems like a good time.' J takes the bong back, and packs one for himself.

I get excited, 'hell no, of course I don't mind. Your trip - your rules.'

'All I'm saying is we gonna have a group trip this time, not just us you know?'

'It's all good. Make the arrangements. I better book my flight back then I guess.' I look around nervously for my passport to sort the details out.

J focuses on the telly again and picks up his game of *Wipeout* (PS1). J calm as ever, 'cool, no worries.'

I go into the other room and ruffle some paper from my bag, then dial a number in the kitchen. J remains sitting in the living room alone for the time being, the bong sits on the table expelling smoke slowly from the previous hit. He looks around the room one last time, and gets a slight shiver. He shakes his head, and switches off the PlayStation and the TV on for a welcome distraction. Behind him stands a dark shadowy figure. It is the ghost of our dead Dad paying him a visit from the *in-between world*.

．

The next day I wait for my brother downstairs on the front door step. Korn's *No Place* plays in my mind, and I nod my head to the beat and attempt singing along. Flashes of the train terrorist hi-jacking pop in and out of my head. Am I crazy? Am I imagining these things that aren't real? Are they flashes to the future? J comes stomping down the stairs behind me, and I react by getting up shaking off my *visions*.

CHAPTER 5 - ARIZONA

I sit outside on our patio as William Orbit's *Hinterland 3* is playing on my stereo; it's the song where the narrator tells the story of Lorraine on Mantauk Point. Lyrics of the song play in my head. 'And Lorraine sat out on the porch, in the rain, to smoke a joint. She had a smile on her face that made her look a little crazy.'

I always connected with this song for some reason, and it isn't just because we share the same name. It is the night I've arrived back in the States and I sit alone on my Mom's porch/patio smoking a joint by myself. I recall the cricket sounds when I was tripping in Dam and associating it with the cicadas at night over here. They were always there but I blocked them out of my mind until now.

My Mom appears at the fly-screen door; she doesn't say anything but simply watches me at first for a moment. I sense her presence and turn towards her briefly. Mom stands there watching me for a while. I put the joint in the ashtray. She comes out behind the screen door and sits next to me.

'It's OK honey, I was just thinking about your Dad and your brother.'

I cough quietly, 'what about em?'

She continues, 'how they didn't see each other for ages. It's a shame that's all. He didn't get to say bye.'

'J says he's cool with what happened, he's made his peace.'

Mom sadly replies, 'that's good, I suppose.' After a long pause my Mom walks back into the house closing the screen door.

I look back at her for a bit longer listening to the shuffling footsteps of my depressed mother. She still loved my Dad even years after their separation. I turn to the ashtray once more and pick up the joint and light it again. I take a couple deep puffs, nearly coughing. My eyes glaze over, I'm definitely stoned again now.

The wake comes and goes, family members cry and feast. I keep to myself in a corner most of the time. People offer me their condolences I nod but don't say much. I sneak out at one point to take a couple hits on a pipe. I miss my Dad but more than that I think of London and more importantly of Holland. I feel like there is unfinished business to be attended to and can't wait till I get back to that (trippin) world once more.

Burning Man Festival at the end of the summer, the massive salt plain is filled with hippies and druggies alike. I have been invited last minute and have wanted to attend this festival my whole life. Now I'm finally here expanding my mind some more.

At night I sit among some of my friends, yet I'm distant from the conversation and fun going on around me. I'm tripping on some Acid and it is the night of the festival that someone lights the *Wicker Man* prematurely before the end of the week.

I'm sitting around a big camp fire spacing out, reflecting on my life and my family situation. Josh, one of my friends pulls me up; I get up eventually and am forced to dance, even though I can't stand for long. After trying to do couple of dance moves, I collapse back into my seat. I decide to lie down on a makeshift carpet. I look up at the stars and see them moving in sync with the jamming drum session happening nearby and bass in the background.

The next morning my friends and I are still recovering after the heavy night, as the sun rises on the horizon. Some are sleeping in the jeep, a couple others in their tents, even a few slept outside, covering themselves with some thin material and makeshift blankets. I wake up in the boot of a friend's van, and I step out still mildly tripping since its early morning and I barely slept. The come down. A small fire's coals glisten slightly in the wind. I stretch and put on a hoody, whipping my dreads out I tie them up with a piece of random string. I take out my sunglasses and climb up the van to sit on top with a lightweight chair. I sit for a moment and skin up a small joint. I look towards the sun, from time to time seeing somebody in our camp stirring or awake. As I take a deep drag, I place my *sunnys* on my head and try opening my eyes a bit. It brings back the mild hallucinations for a while. I can see energy fields in the sky; they look like *fractals,* an organized tribal puzzle of some kind. It moves slowly as if in sync with my breathing. I can't believe what I'm seeing. I try my newfound technique over and over then eventually I pass out again, this time in the sun! I ended up sunburnt in my face. I'm glad I came but it's not the same as tripping with my brother. My friend's feel that I have been a bit distant compared to my usual happy bubbly self. A couple days after that day we head back to *the world*.

CHAPTER 6 - DAMNED

J and I are finally together again walking the streets of Amsterdam. We arrived separately so had to have a meeting point. We meet up together then get to the next meeting point to hook up with Kay and the London crew. As they approach a fountain in a square, I spot Kay sitting with a couple of guys. Kay immediately gets up to greet her long lost *sister*. We embrace as girls do when they haven't seen each other for a while.

Kay starts the chat with, 'how are you girlfriend?'

I simply say, 'you know just chilling like always.'

'Chillin, huh? Well we gonna do some chillin over the next few days I tell ya.'

The two guys she was waiting with stand close by waiting for introductions. China stands further forward than Jack, who lingers shyly in the back. Kay turns to J and they kiss briefly, as the guys step closer and offer their hands for a handshake. I simply make a fist and they quickly change their hand to a fist too. Kay turns towards them and apologizes.

Kay realises she hasn't made the introductions yet, 'sorry about that, China this is Lorraine.' China nods. He is an Asian type, he seems quite chilled.

I correct Kay, 'call me Lo.'

'Yeah oops, Lo. True dat.'

China speaks up, 'hi, I'm China. How was your trip? You live in the States right?'

'Yeah just temporarily though. I'm moving to London after this trip. I'm starting film school. I got accepted a couple months ago.'

'Cool. Also, this is Jack,' China says turning around.

Jack steps forward and offers his fist too.

I make contact, and then burst out with, 'yo can we get a smoke now. I've been gagging for one for two days now.'

We all start walking as a group, and we all have our bags over our shoulders.

Kay has a plan, 'I know a good one close by, we can prob get shrooms from there too. We gotta be outta here in an hour though. Our train leaves at four.'

I ask after hearing her talk, 'is it me or have you learned some more US slang?'

'Ah, you noticed, eh? Yeah, it's China here, he loves American movies.'

'Yeah I love da gangsta movie.' China happy to chip in.

I go along with it, 'you mean like Scarface and Al Capone huh?'

He replies, 'no way man. Da black gangsta movie. Like Snoop Doggy and other rappers.'

I laugh and enlighten China with some info, 'you do know they ain't real gangsters right? They like all have kids and shit now.'

'Real for me, no problem.'

'Heh, whatever floats your boat bro.'

China comes back with, 'ahhh, I like that. Whateva floats yo boat. Cool.' He repeats it to himself a couple times.

I turn to my brother, who is holding Kay's hand as they stroll along. 'Bro, this ain't gonna be nothing like last time.'

J replies 'It'll be cool, trust me. You'll see.'

Jack is Caucasian, French-Canadian, polite and a druggie too. Jack comes up alongside me trying to make conversation, since I'm a girl he automatically expects me to be interested in him.

'So you and J been here in Dam before I heard.'

I look toward my bro for help, 'yeah something like that. What about you? How often you trip?'

Jack tells her of the previous night, 'well I stayed here last night even before you guys got here. I had a kinda weird one to be honest.'

'I'm always keen to hear any tripping stories. Go

ahead.'

Jack takes a deep breath. 'I was tripping by myself and I had a bad one. I thought I was gonna die. I stared at myself in the mirror for hours since I couldn't figure out how to get out of the bathroom. My face fell off and all I could see was -'

'- dude, that's not cool!'

J speaks up, 'yeah what the fuck? You didn't have to bring that up now, you know.'

Jack apologetically, 'sorry, I was just making conversation.'

I give him a funny look now, getting slightly creeped out by the story. I was in a great mood until just then.

Outside the *Tongan Surfer* coffee shop our group stop and get ready to buy the goods which will last us the next few days.

Kay holds up her arms and smiles widely. 'OK mo-fos, this is the place.'

J raises his voice, 'OK guys, let's stock up shall we.'

J holds the door open for every one as they file in one by one. Once inside it is more of a stall than a café; but we are there to purchase, not to chill.

We come across the seller and question him about the various mushies in packages with descriptions of the shrooms inside. He has them all laid out on the counter in front of us: a variety of Mexican, Thai and a new one we had never heard of before: *Copelandia*. They look like small grey liberty caps from England, but not. You need loads of UK shrooms even for a mild trip. We are not here for mild, you dig?

The seller informs us, 'you have the usual but these ones new. I've heard they very strong. So careful not to mix, ja.'

J picks up the packaging, not impressed, 'they look pretty tiny to me bro. Kinda remind me of UK liberty caps. Weak as hell and you need loads of em.'

The seller leans closer to make sure we understand. 'Your choice man, believe me I heard they real strong. Don't underestimate ze power ja.'

J buys all of them and finishes the deal with, 'whatever. We can give em a go. Fuck it, why not?'

They exchange money, the rest of us buy ours after.

Next we head towards Amsterdam Central station ready for the train journey. Along the way J and I take some shrooms on the sly reaching into our small packets and taking out mini doses too eager to wait. Plus the train ride might be kinda boring too.

Inside the train cabins China and Jack sit together, while J, Kay, and I sit by the windows. I'm fiddling with my camera, having come up slightly already when the others notice that I brought something to document this *historic trip*. I clip on a wide angle lens converter and plug in a small microphone.

I ask out loud, 'I hope you guys don't mind, but I'm gonna be doin' some filmin' over the next few days.'

Everybody shrugs no, after giving each other a confirmation look each.

I then hand the mic to Jack and press record on my camera. 'So Jack, tell me a little about yourself.'

Jack takes a deep breath looking from side to side, not used to being put on the spot; he is a tad paler too now. After a long pause and clearing his throat, 'there's not much to tell. Sometimes I feel like I have a voice in my head, telling me to do things. But I'm pretty sure I got it under control, I think.'

'Why don't you tell us about last night?'

Jack ponders – 'last night. Well I had sex with a black prostitute while I was tripping, and afterwards I saw there was a hole in the rubber.'

China chuckles out loud, finding this amusing, not seeing the potential lethal risk of this event. 'You jackass! You gonna have baby boy. You gonna be a Daddy. Ha ha!'

Jack defensively, 'shut up China. It wasn't cool, it freaked me out man. I started tripping proper afterwards. I took the shrooms to get me in the mood. So later on I'm by myself in the mirror and my face is literally peeling off. And if I'd touch my skin, dude it would come right off.'

J decisively steps in, 'we don't need to know all the details OK. Don't you fuckin bring up that tripping story again!' He looks away again out the window disgusted since he has come up also by now.

'Heh, she asked me man!' Jack defensively.

I get serious again for my *potential film project.* 'OK, enough already. I'll move on to the next contestant.' I pan the camera in China's direction.

China laughs again to himself unaware of the camera yet.

J looks at him, and smirks a little, then looks out the window again. Kay has cuddled up to him with her feet on the seat.

I keep filming this whole time, but now focus on China for the next interview. I wave for Jack to pass the microphone.

'So how's your sex life China?'

Put on the spot China gets all serious, then straightens up to look sensible and respectable for some reason. He wipes his hair and stops smiling.

'Ha! My sex life is fine, thank you. And I don't need prostitute,' looking over at Jack while he says this.

Jack gives him an evil look, and then crosses his arms looking away.

I sarcastically ask, 'oh yeah? You some kind of sex stud, are ya?'

'Yeah man. Me like sex god.' China thinks he's pretty cool. Everybody starts laughing, including Jack.

'Yeah, uh huh. Whatever dude,' Jack has his revenge temporarily in his mind.

China continues, 'me like Mack Daddy, James Bond.'

Kay tries to change the conversation, not really caring about the discussion.

Instead my bro changes tactics and conversation, 'hate to rain on your guys' parade, but to business. What shrooms you get? I was thinking we could trade and mix and match or something.'

I turn the camera towards him but also ready to join the conversation. Half filming and half spaced out.

J starts the bids, whipping out his various bags, 'some *Thai*; big fuckers. The guy at the shop said one would be enough. Then we also got some *Copelandia*; small but potent. On top of that we got some *Mexican* too.'

The *Thai* and *Mexican* are definitely the largest out of the lot. I jokingly remark, 'I think we got enough for a regiment.' I chuckle whilst starting to trip.

Kay sarcastically, the unofficial Mom of the group, 'I don't think were gonna be running out any time soon.'

J nonchalantly, 'you know me; I always need more than everyone else.'

'I'll take that challenge, good sir.' My attempt at a fake UK accent.

'B and B mate? Breakfast lunch and dinner?' J gives the accent a go too again. LOL.

I go back to my normal voice. 'Why don't I doubt that? You should have seen us last time. How much did we take? I lost count.' Literally trying to count in my head with no such luck.

J all business-man like and back to his real voice, 'another thing, the guy that sold them, told us not to mix (all of) them. And not to underestimate the *Copelandia*. He nearly didn't want to sell us the lot all at once. But Dutch will be Dutch.'

'Did you just really say that?' Kay smirks and gives him a kiss on the cheek.

J continues, 'I told him we were splitting it up evenly over a few days.'

'Whatever it takes huh?' I agree nodding.

'Whatever it takes sista.'

J and I do high fives then in a flash I see a faint resemblance of a skull in Kay's facial features. Is it the shadows of her cheek bones or something else? I shrug it off and peer out the window spacing out, watching the flat landscape outside the train window. I'm already thinking of the evening ahead, blocking this part out of my memory for now. I put my camera away, plug in my headphones and listen to some Primus' *Bob's Party*.

CHAPTER 7 - NOWHERE

We have all made it to Kay's family country house a few hours outside Amsterdam. Fast forward to everyone choosing a room, dumping our stuff until everyone settles in the lounge area. We have a large wooden dinner table, two couches, an open window and best of all: a fireplace. Tripping never gets boring as long as there's a fire around. It's not like I'm a *pyromaniac* or anything, just something to watch and trip out to plus being a crazy heat source to boot. It is dark outside already now and we are all tripping.

Umma Gumma by Pink Floyd plays on the stereo as I try to film as much as possible but put the camera on a mini tripod every now and then. Jack is crawling around on the floor, including under the table. China is laughing his ass off in a chair in the corner. J is trying to keep Kay awake, she keeps drifting off. As high as the peak, equally is the low when the drugs start to wear off. It is a constant battle to stay awake at the end of a trip late at night.

J sees Jack under the table both of them laughing at the situation. 'What the fuck are you doing Jack? You crazy, man.'

Jack in return answers with a weird noise/growl followed by intense screaming combined with laughing.

China is holding his hands up in the air, as if fondling something. I see this and pick up my camera and start to film him. He doesn't notice I'm filming since he has his eyes shut. He is caressing some imaginary being in front of him.

From behind my camera, 'what do you see China? What do you feel?'

China still with his eyes closed, 'me so horny. I see naked women everywhere.'

I finally get why he has his hands in that position now, I zoom in and notice he is licking his lips. Getting slightly creeped out yet fascinated by this scenario since remember I'm a part-time lesbian. 'OOOOKKKKKKK. Describe what you see. How many do you see?'

China continues as if in a trance still unaware he's being filmed. 'Many women, they are everywhere.'

I'm giggling to myself now and then Jack appears alongside me, still on all fours. I pan towards the floor but the auto focus is switching constantly back and forth. Cheap ass built-in lens.

'Where? Where? I wanna see naked women everywhere too.'

Since Jack generally has darker trips than China he wants a piece of the action, in this case. China has his hands at his side now, as if fondling girls on either side.

My lens focus turns its attention back and forth between Jack and China. Then I get real close to his face to see how close I can get without being noticed. I also capture a moment of Jack looking at China with fascination. Jack looks up at me, asking if he can do some filming. I hand him my camera slowly, trusting this *person* with my future.

'You drop it, you're dead. Got it?' I remind him just in case.

Jack takes it gratefully, 'yeah, cool, please I'll be careful.'

I stay and watch him for a bit, making sure he knows what he's doing. Jack really gets into filming China; I think he has hopes of maybe catching naked women on camera somehow.

China is still in his hallucination, 'wow, tits everywhere. Me so horny.'

Jack taking on the documentary film-maker director type, 'describe em to me dude.'

'They so huge and round. So cool.' China continues fondling imaginary tits in mid-air.

Kay wakes up groggily and stands up disgusted by China and his behaviour. Kay with a new bout of energy decisively turns to J and says, 'let's go upstairs baby. I wanna lie down. This is too much.'

J replies 'calm down babe. Let me skin up then we can go. I told you not to sleep yet; we gotta last out the trip. It's trying to make us tired, you have to fight it.'

Kay sits back down defeated, but waiting till her other half comes to his senses and takes her upstairs. She won't go by herself, afraid something might happen without him there to protect her.

I come over to the table and sit down next to my brother. While we are both skinning up I make small talk. 'So you got any hallucinations yet bro?

'Nah, not properly. I'm totally tripping though.'

I continue enjoying this little chat, half keeping an eye on Jack with my camera. 'Man I still haven't had full on hallucinations yet. I think I saw an energy field back in the States. At Burning Man festival.'

'Cool, cool. What'd it look like?'

I continue with my experience, 'like a giant organic grid, moving as if it was alive or something. It kinda reminded of waves in the ocean.'

At that exact moment riot police kick down the front door and come into the room with their guns drawn aimed at everyone's heads. They came in so fast; no one has a chance to react. I lean back in my seat as if having a heart attack; I'm as stiff as a log. I look around and no one seems to notice that the cops are standing right in front of them screaming in Dutch.

The Dutch cops shout their commands 'get on the ground now! Hands over your heads! You're all under arrest!'

This goes on for a few seconds. I look around the room and see no one else reacting. Even J keeps rolling his joint during this flash of distorted time. When all of a sudden I snap back into reality with a jolt. This was just like that other vision, what does it mean? First sober now tripping, I can't explain it.

J notices me flinch and surprised asks, 'you OK siss? What happened?'

I'm stunned but don't wanna say too much, 'uhhhhh. I think I might have just had my first one.' I lie.

'One what?' J half looking up at her whilst licking the sticky on the king size Rizla paper.

I explain, 'visual, vision. Whatever you wanna call it.'

J looks concerned, 'you've gone completely white, what did you see?'

I'm shaking with paranoia now, 'cops, Dutch riot police or something. Man that felt so real.'

J calms my nerves, 'cool, join the club. Look you gonna be alright we're gonna go upstairs for a bit. Knock on the door if there's any problems. Sweet?'

Kay is waiting patiently at the door frame waiting until she can go upstairs and chill in private with her lover.

I shrug him off, 'whatever bro. Do what you gotta do.' Obviously I want him to stay.

J holds out his fist, I answer with mine. As J and Kay leave the room, I feel sad being left alone-ish. I finish skinning up a joint for myself since the table is covered in skunk, hash, papers, tobacco, roaches and still a few bags of shrooms. It takes a while, since everything is moving now. I'm still a bit freaked about my first *real* scary *hallucination*; I ponder why I saw what I did. I play out the scenario in my head again thinking of possible reasons within my imagination. The paranoia has mostly faded completely now.

After a while I look over at Jack and China. I can't see clearly what's going on the other side of the room since my focus keeps going in and out. I get closer, first stopping by the stereo and changing the cassette tape to Grateful Dead's *Spaces*. China is passing out now, and Jack is filming the fire a bit too close for my liking. He keeps sticking his arm in and burns off his arm hair. A spark sends him flying backwards out of fear. That's when I decide he's filmed enough; I go over and snatch my camera back.

'What the hell you doing? Are you mad?' I rant.

Jack apologetically, 'I'm sorry I couldn't help it.'

I continue my inquiry, 'from over there it looked like you were putting your arm in the fire. Why would you do that?'

'I wasn't trying to hurt your camera promise,' he looks all innocent and bashful.

I inspect my camera to make sure it still works and isn't burned or damaged. Jack looks up at me like a little child. I am more forgiving now, 'fine, I believe you. But it's not gonna happen again, OK!'

Jack snaps back at me - 'I said I was sorry.'

I turn and walk back to the table and mumble, 'it was those damn voices again was it?' I didn't care if he heard me or not. Thinking about Jack, I decide he's not totally normal and to be weary of him over the next two days.

I astral project for the first time in my life. Upstairs in the master bedroom J and Kay lie in her bed on the opposite side of the house. They have a night light on.

Kay sits up concerned, 'did you hear that?'

J mumbles something lying on his side.

Kay shakes J while leaning over him.

Still tripping he mumbles, 'it's nothing, go back to sleep. Sleep good.' Sounding like a caveman.

'It's just I remember what you said happened last time, when you were in Amsterdam together. I'm worried something like it might happen again.' I guess he had to tell her sometime.

J opens his eyes and looks at her, 'I told you not to worry. Lo can take care of herself. She came back last time, yeah.'

Kay puts her hand on his chest as she says, 'I can't help feel responsible you know. She is like a little sister to me.'

J tries to kiss her to take her mind off of downstairs. She moves away, sitting up on the bed. She puts one of her sweaters and stands up.

Kay, not so burnt out and sleepy anymore, 'I'm gonna go check on them. She is one girl amongst two crazy horny boys.'

J snorts turning back on his side, 'fine, go check if you want. I'm staying here. See ya if you get back in one peace.' He laughs a stereotypical horror laugh.

'Shut up. What's that supposed to mean?'

J chuckles to himself not answering her question. Kay puts on her slippers then slowly creeps down the stairs. She can hear distorted muffled noises. Some incoherent dialogue, mixed with groans. She is down the stairs now and peers around the corner seeing movement but can't quite make it out. Hearing China snoring in the corner, she steps into the room cautiously thinking it's safe. She can see Jack on the floor hugging his knees in fear, she is about to go to help him when out of nowhere I grab her from behind. Literally acting and looking like a zombie. I guess it's all those *zombie apocalypse* dreams I have, once a month on average.

Kay screams and falls to the ground out of fright. I have a distorted face and move like the undead. I groan like in the movies, coming towards Kay flashing my teeth. Kay gets up to run out of the room. I can't control myself I'm absorbed by whatever weird trip I'm having that night. As soon as she leaves I stop being a zombie (including making the noises) and just stand motionless. A bit like in *I am Legend* with Will Smith when the zombies sleep standing up breathing really fast.

Moments later Kay peeks round the door to see where I am. Standing in the middle of the room, I turn towards Kay only when she comes in the room then I become a motionless zombie again. It's as if I'm *activated* by Kay's presence in the room, but I can't leave the room either. I'm stuck in the trip.

Kay has had enough, still tripping slightly herself she runs back upstairs into the arms of her caring boyfriend. Kay is shaking because of the shock. She seeks J's arms under the covers. J comes back to reality then drifting off for a bit. She then shakes him awake properly disturbing his peaceful in-between tripping and dreaming moments some refer to as *Mescalin*.

J holding her tight, 'shhhhhh. It's alright I'm here. I told you not to go didn't I?'

'She was a frickin' zombie J!'

'Who? What you talking about?'

Kay snaps - 'your sister. Your fuckin sister man! Is she crazy like for real crazy?'

J awake now, 'what you saying? So she flipped a switch a year ago, happens to everyone sooner or later. Tripping makes people do stupid shit sometimes, you know that.'

Kay, biting her nails. 'I know, but you always hear those stories of people getting stuck in a trip.'

'Sometimes, not to us though. I don't know; maybe she is a little bit.'

'You should know; she's your sister.' Kay smacks him gently.

J comforts her, 'she's just havin fun. Look, you'll forgive her tomorrow once were sober, OK?'

Kay confirms, 'fine, she better be alright, you hear me?'

'Yeah, yeah. Whatever, try and get some sleep will you. Forget about downstairs. You're safe up here.'

'Love you Jay.' She seeks love to make sure they are still partners in this relationship.

He concurs, 'love you too babe.'

It is the next morning. J and Kay snoop around looking for some breakfast. She raids the cupboards and discovers some tinned food. J finds a seat by the counter and starts rolling a wake-and-bake joint. The smell of skunk wafts into the living room waking up Jack and China, who have remained in the living room passed out until now.

I stir in my sleep upstairs hearing sounds of chatter and laughter downstairs. I try to sleep but can't, so I get dressed and head downstairs. A Dutch radio station plays quietly in the background. Everyone looks a little tired and *zombie-fied*. Especially when I enter the room, everyone makes a cheering sound. I plomp down at the kitchen table and slump my head down attempting to rest my eyes still. Jack eyes me cautiously only remembering bits and pieces of the previous night.

China helps Kay cook some cheese on toast with some eggs.

J passes me a joint, I take it reluctantly at first. A couple of hits later I offer it to the room.

Jack comes over and takes it off me slowly, just in case. He remembers being afraid of me, but I can't remember why at this stage.

Kay looks over at us in concern.

Jack trying to flirt a little, 'that was a pretty heavy night there Lo. I might miss out on tonight, you can have my shrooms if you want. I'm damn wrecked I tell ya.'

'I'll take em. Whatever you guys don't want is not goin to waste if I can help it. Lo, back me up here.' My bro answers for me. J is testing me to see if I'm up for two hard-core nights in a row or will it make me crack for good.

I just grumble to myself, not quite able to formulate a conversation this early. I try to remember last night but can't focus on anything. Can't remember any zombies yet.

China joins the conversation, 'yeah me too bro. Me not feel too hot, we'll see later. But I'm pretty sure that was enough for me. My tummy is fucked man.'

Jack is happy China is on his side as if creating a divide in the group, 'yeah mine too, it is poison after all.'

I say out loud, 'poison?' Which is long and drawn out as if time is still slightly distorted. Everyone looks over at me to see if there was anything else I was going to say, but no luck.

Kay comes in energetically, 'morning sleepy head. How you feeling? You freaked me out last night. Do you remember anything?'

'Sorry can't remember all of it,' me mumbling the whole time.

J continues, 'well I had an awesome time. And it ain't over yet.'

Jack is adamant, 'it is for me and China. Last night was enough to last a lifetime.'

I'm a bit more coherent now, 'not sure if I can pass, I mean how often we gotta do this shit right?'

'You're kidding right? Did we have a bad trip or was that just me?' Jack is not giving up his *argument*.

I counter with, 'I wouldn't necessarily call it bad. Just fuckin' weird that's all.'

'You were pretty fucked Lo. Is there any footage of you acting like a zombie?'

I ignore this comment for now, 'that's the whole point, right? Isn't that why we're here?'

Jack crosses his arms looking down defeated, 'well it definitely was too intense for me.'

Kay rationalising, 'maybe that's because we all took shit loads.'

J proud of this, 'damn straight.'

China is recalling bits and pieces now, 'I remember naked women. Did we go to strip club or somethin?'

'Where? Out in the middle of nowhere?' J sarcastically remarks.

Kay assuming the mother-hen role again, 'we stayed right here China, I think it's safe to say we all hallucinated something. So who's coming for a walk then?'

J, 'I'll come yo.'

Jack, indecisive, 'I might, maybe. Let me think about it.'

'I think I stay here too.' China adds.

'Lo?'

'Hang on. I gotta have another smoke first. Let me get my camera. Jack, you saw it last, where is it?'

'Me? Why me? You had it.' He feels cornered.

'Did I? Where the fuck did I leave it? China did you see it anywhere?'

China has a flash of the previous night, 'nah, sorry. I only remember naked chicks.'

I squint since it's getting old already, 'yeah we know,

you told us ready like a million times.'

'Sorry,' he slouches.

China, Jack, Kay and J are feeding on bread and makeshift dips.

Kay encourages me to eat, 'Lo, you want some of this?'

I'm the same as other times post-trip, 'not sure. I'll try a bite, maybe some fruit. I feel as hot as everyone else here.'

I stand up and drag my feet over, have a little nibble on a banana. 'Well, there's nothing like wakin and bakin eh guys?' They all nod in agreement, with a couple muffled noises whilst everyone is still eating.

I'm shuffling about in the living room looking for my camera when I find it under a pile of clothes.

The others stay munching on whatever food they can find.

I return to the kitchen. I play some of the footage with sounds echoing through the room. Not concerned with small talk I continue playing with my LCD monitor to piece together the previous night. 'It was on the floor, I hope no one dropped it.'

Jack snaps - 'you might've, just as well as me.'

I'm too spaced out for a fight, 'chill man, I wasn't saying nothing. Let me just check it first before anyone panics.' I fiddle with some switches, beeps can be heard. I sigh out loud for relief and continue, 'thank fuck for that. I didn't even realize it was missing last night.'

Kay breaks the tension, 'none of us checked anything last night. Be thankful it's still working. I'm heading out in five mins if anyone changes their mind.'

Jack and China still nod no; she looks at me one last time.

I look up and am won over by Kay's puppy dog eyes begging me to come with.

'Be ready in five?' J is still rolling his joint.

'Yeah, yeah.'

Kay leaves the room, to brush her teeth upstairs and get

a couple extra bits of clothing.

The other three go to the living room and gather some extra bits of clothes too. Jack and China still deciding whether to come for a walk.

When she comes back down, Kay and J put on some wellington boots. She looks over at me while I stare out the window. Kay noticing this and tries to get me involved in the group again. 'Let's get some fresh air guys; after all we will be spending another night here again tomorrow.'

We all agree and get up one by one preparing ourselves for the outside world. Despite some grumbles we head out the front door.

It's cloudy outside; there is also a grey mist in the fields. Our druggie group wonder the local country paths. Everyone still on quite the come down from the previous night, stumble past random dog walkers. Kay even says hello to some neighbours as they pass along the way. In that state J and I wish we could just go right back to the house, get stoned and maybe even start tripping again. For now we bear the fresh air with yet more boring flat landscape surrounding us all.

CHAPTER 8 - THE TRIP

Later that night China and Jack get comfy by the fire. I sit at the main table and skin up a fat joint for me and the boys. After I pass it, I rewind the tape to the beginning and plug it into a small TV on some shelves. As it plays in black & white China and Jack watch bits and pieces, but there is no sound. The only sounds heard in the room are a grandfather clock ticking, the fire sparking and the Dutch radio left on in the kitchen. On the TV China is being filmed (by Jack), they both laugh out loud. They talk while watching.

Jokingly I say, 'you were getting into those naked ladies quite a bit there Jack.'

'So, what if I was? I'm a guy in case you hadn't noticed.'

'It's all good, it's natural right. In my case I like girls too you know.'

Jack turns to China, 'see! I told you China, I knew she was a lesbian.'

'Coooool,' is his response.

'Well it's not that simple. I haven't actually had many experiences but I do prefer it to be honest.' I decide to be open up this one time.

'Sick, that's awesome yo.' Jack is supportive.

China shares a bit of his past, 'I had girlfriend once, she dumped me and became lesbian. She say girls always more attracted to other women than men.'

Jack mocks him, 'sucks for you dude. Missing out I say.'

China continuing, 'we had one experience. I got some ecstasy and we party together then we end up in bed, the three of us. After that she never have sex with me no more. She leave me.'

'Sorry dude. I didn't mean to stir up any old memories.'

'It's OK, it was best night of my life. Then the shittest time after that. Why she do that to me man?' China sulking as he says this.

Jack gives his two pence, 'you want a serious answer?'

I'm sympathetic towards China, leaning in. 'What Jack should be saying is don't worry, you'll get some again . . . sometime that is.'

'It's not the end of world bro. Chicks screw guys over all the time.'

'And vice versa bro.' I even the odds.

Jack, sarcastically putting on a mock UK accent, 'sorry your honour. I move for a vote of no confidence.'

I temporarily become a Judge and wave towards the prosecutor, 'motion granted. Enough talk for now huh?'

We sit quietly watching the random footage, sometimes very shaky.

Then China bursts out with, 'man I just thought something. Jay and Lo means J-Lo, Jennifer Lopez get it? And Jay and Kay equals J-Kay, Jamiroquai. That's so cool guys.'

OK we nod, since it's pretty random information, but totally true also. Then J and Kay come back into the room to see what's on TV. Kay not interested, disappears into the house to read peacefully somewhere. J sticks around skinning up. Time passes and bags of shrooms are being ripped open and J and I start *caning* the shrooms again.

Fast forward a couple hours as the trips start to take their effect again. China and Jack sit still in the same chairs as in the afternoon not indulging. They haven't moved, passing out regularly, waking up briefly when a loud laugh is heard or some commotion is made. The video footage from the camera is no longer playing, the tape ended a while back. Kay, J, and I are splitting up the last of the shrooms equally. J and I have bigger portions than Kay.

We sit around the other TV, this time with colour and sound. J and Kay rustle around in the bags picking and choosing which ones they're gonna eat. They leave the rest with me. I offer the left-overs one last time to Jack and China but they grovel and decline, holding their stomachs in pain. I laugh out loud to myself and not even realizing it but already start piling random shrooms in my mouth not even checking which are which. I feel the power trip coming back from our first trip to Dam. I feel stronger than before and my come down is long gone for now.

J breaks the silence with, 'yo, we're gonna head up stairs, you kids behave now you hear.' Chuckling to himself since they have come up too already. J and Kay are supporting each other as they stumble/crawl up the stairs with their arms around their shoulders.

Jack and China murmur some grunts, not able to form full words.

I look around at the two guys passing out, grinning tilting my head back slowly, then upright instantly. I can't believe me being the youngest and still going strong after a night of proper tripping already. The TV is showing *Leaving Las Vegas* it has been playing the whole time, and is slowly coming to an end. It is in English with Dutch subtitles. I try to focus on what's going on, it's the end now where Nicholas Cage is dying in bed, and Elisabeth Shue (his angel) straddles him for one last time. Since nothing else is going on, I'm focused on the emotions coming from the TV screen. I even cry a bit, getting into the film all over again, yet seeing it through slightly different (tripping) eyes this time.

As the film ends visuals start to appear around the TV, the frame remains constant throughout though. The walls start moving and colours are shifting between mainly orange and green. I start moving around in my seat slightly feeling a case of excitement. All of a sudden, I pass out without even realizing it happened.

Complete blackness and silence. Slowly trippy tracers start to appear from top to bottom. It seems I'm sinking or drifting down similarly to the bottom of an ocean of darkness. The tracers fade as my hallucinations continue, while my POV reveals a large hall/room which stretches to infinity in every direction. An infinite space. It seems to stretch for miles yet bits and pieces start to come into focus in the foreground. The colours continue to consist of orange and green, film grain is everywhere in my vision. Depth of field plays tricks on my mind as I look around trying to look at my surroundings. I can hear dance music but not yet clearly. I hear a Dutch voice way off in the distance, but no person to match it with as it echoes around this *purgatory*.

Way up above is a timer clock which is a time-code (eg. 0:0:20:12). It is counting down to or from something, I can't tell which. I stare at it trying to figure it out, but this is before film school, before I knew what time-code was. I look up and down at this giant space, where did it come from all of a sudden? My head feels like a weight, so I look to my left side. I'm shocked at what I see . . . it's me! Looking back at myself too, it is moving exactly the same as I am as if a mirror image. The only way to describe it is when an infinity mirror is in front and behind you it seems to stretch forever getting smaller the further away. Not only this, but my *twins* extend to the end of this infinite space.

The music becomes clearer and louder now, the track turns into a dark drum and bass song that my mind has literally made up in the trip. Creeped out by the sounds and sight I squeeze my eyes shut and open them looking the other way. Same thing! I look straight ahead hoping that my *image* will disappear on its own. It doesn't; instead a list starts appearing in front of me below the time-code stretching to the floor. It is like a print read out or a computer screen scanning for viruses. The (rap sheet) list consists of dates and offences, ie smoking, masturbating, drinking alcohol, having sex, etc. I try to read it but the list is going by too fast for me to focus, in this state anyway. I catch a few glimpses of dates I clearly remember like my birthday, Christmas, and New Year's. I'm pretty sure the information is completely accurate, how this other place would know such information is still a mystery to me. I guess it's because it's my subconscious, which has always been present in my waking life.

A Dutch news reporter can be heard but still not seen. "Today's news. Another young victim has died tonight of a magic mushroom overdose. Lorraine Kingston was a promising art student, who was about to enter film school next year. She showed talent, possibly leading to a successful career in the film business. Leaving behind her family in America, and her brother and friends who found her body. She, like many others had fallen into the trap of Dutch tourism. Coming here for the legal highs has resulted in her fatal choice of drugs. Now to other news."

By the end of the report I feel like I have understood the message despite being in a foreign language. A sense of real dread starts to build inside me. Hearing my name and some words that sounded familiar I piece together the report. Before I know it, the middle-aged bald newsman with big 80's glasses is sitting on my lap. Literally - no jokes. It's as if it's a 3-D holographic image on my lap, the rest of the TV is nowhere to be seen. So for a moment it's as if the reporter is talking to me directly since the screen is pretty much in front of me. I'm starting to get scared and try to claw myself away from him, but I can't stand up or move out of my seat, as if held or weighed down somehow. I look around to see if anyone can help, but there is no one except for my *clones*, only the sound of distant snoring mixed with the Dutch newsman carrying on with his other *real* reports. I even try to brush him away, with no effect. My hands simply go through him.

Banging in the distance has gotten louder and louder. A shadowy form appears coming from left to right on a loop. It is a large soldier like cartoon figure (silhouette) with no features, like an angry ghost coming back for revenge of some sort. He continues appearing and disappearing at first, just stomping by in front of me. I hope at first that it won't notice me but then it starts turning towards me and facing me again in a loop. Each time it seems to change and become more aggressive, the sounds of its colossal boots making the banging louder the closer it gets. Its arms begin to form into tentacles (*Deep Rising* film influence), like weapons attacking me while I'm trapped on the couch. Despite the randomness of this vision it appears to work mathematically in the loop with exact timing. Each moment it comes back it is eating part of me away. As if scanning or printing through me, I literally feel parts of my body being eaten away bit by bit. I lean back into the couch more and more as time goes by. I cannot stand having lost the ability to use my legs what seemed like hours ago. The soldier-like creature continues to eat away at my physical body. The whole time the drum and bass track plays loudly in my mind's eye. Eventually the trip settles down slowly. I pass out or not, I'm not quite sure.

Next thing I notice is my body is completely flat (like Holland's landscape) with my head sticking out like a loose balloon being blown around in the wind. One of the last things I remember is seeing the globe rotating on its axis, space surrounding it. I calm down momentarily, as if finally peace fills me after hours of torture. It is the stillness of outer space that calms the storm. Then all of a sudden nuclear explosions begin to appear around this mini globe. They appear small on the image, but I know that they are devastating, spreading slowly all over. They are most likely in or around major cities, since I can tell one side is black/dark because of night-time. I can see the detail of city lights (the grid) lit then vanish with the nukes, as if they had taken out power grids all over the planet. This is another heavy blow to me, since I just came out of this crazy trip, then a moment's pause and all hell breaks loose again. I'm blown away, with the blasts. In shock, I look down at the ground in depression.

The walls of visuals are breaking down slightly and bits of the living room can be seen as if through ghostly images. I notice my brother's coconut bong sitting on the floor next to my right leg. Happiness appears in my face for the first time in hours, I am relieved to know I can at least smoke weed if I'm stuck in hell/purgatory. I take a massive hit, bigger than usual and just like that the visual wall falls completely apart like a veil being lifted/dropped. So happy to be back in the real world I jump out of my seat, pat myself up and down to check if it's still my body, next I look around the room to see if anyone else is there.

I can't see China anywhere; he must have snuck off to a couch or a bed. However, Jack is passed out on the same couch as before *the trip*. Immediately I go over to wake him up, shaking him to make sure he is alive. You never can be too sure.

'Jack! Jack, can you see me? Tell me if I'm alive.'

Jack rubbing his eyes, 'wha? Yeah of course I can see you. Why'd you wake me up?'

'Sorry, I had to tell someone, anyone about this amazing trip I just had. I mean it was baaaaaddd, but at the same time the most intense visuals ever!'

Jack opens his eyes wider and looks up at me properly for the first time since his rude awakening. It's then that I notice something weird. Jack's eyes are black! Freaked out not sure if I'm still tripping, alive or if my sub-conscious is still messing with me like twists in certain movies. I back away from him slowly. Still on the hyperactive buzz, I dart into the other room. 'Laters.'

I look around and see China curled up in a chair by the dead fire. He looks like a little hibernating mouse. I pace over and wake him up too, more gently this time, just in case he's got *black eyes* too. When China opens his eyes, I carefully inspect them to make sure. It's safe and I go into more detail about the trip since China's eyes aren't scaring me like Jack's did.

I'm quite hyper now as if being *trapped* for hours has given me new life and energy.

'Sorry to wake you man, but I just had to tell you about what happened in this trip I came out of. I'm so happy to be here, to be alive I mean. I thought I was dead bro. That's the most intense trip I've ever had, I've never had anything like it. It was pretty crazy at times, or even the whole way through really. It was a bad trip I guess, but I haven't really figured it out yet, you know? I was in fucking purgatory man, I couldn't get out. I was stuck and even at one point I was flat! Can you believe it?'

China is trying to stay awake but still burned out and mega tired he nods off half way through towards the ends of my story. I didn't even notice that he passed out because I was so into telling the story, it was like a part of me was still there. Similar to when you've just out of a dream, and still half in *that* world. Realizing he's not listening anymore, I quietly get up and go over to the *drug table* and skin up a joint to take up stairs. It takes me a while, trying to *focus* and not fuckin up the roll. When I'm done, I sneak past Jack in the other room and head up stairs.

J and Kay are naked under the covers; the night light is always on since Kay can't sleep without it. I poke my head into the room, I light up the joint and whisper.

'Sssspppppt J! You awake?'

He rolls over and mumbles something but doesn't open his eyes yet. He licks his lips, clearing the dryness in his throat also.

'What? Lo, that you? What's up? Is that a joint I smell? Gimme some.'

I pass the joint, still pretty happy, 'here ya go. Heh listen. I just had the sickest trip ever yo. I already told Jack and China, but they pretty much passed out now. So I came up here to tell ya.'

J not really caring but goes on about his trip now, 'I had a mad trip too. I can remember being born. I was inside Kay's womb, and I came out into the world. It was so real, I can even remember being born for real.'

Kay giggles to herself on the other side of the bed knowing what they were really up to in the previous hours.

'Great! You're tripping about being reborn, I get the death trip, is that it?'

I look up at the ceiling/sky for God to answer, but I'm too busy getting into my side of the story now. I continue excitedly, 'like I was saying I took way too much, I didn't even keep track of what I was having after a while.'

J opens up his eyes now to check on his kid sister's facial expression.

'Living dangerously there Lo. So is there any left?'

'I'm not sure; you can have em if so. I've taken enough for a life time.'

He reminds me, 'and you're gonna feel it over the next few days too.'

'Well at least now I can enjoy myself. I'm still buzzing man. How much did you take?'

He mumbles – 'I split it with Kay, we finished our bag.'

I contemplate for a moment, 'so we both mixed did we?'

J confirms, 'so much for listening to the guy's advice at the coffee shop.'

I add, 'and what's written on the packs.'

I have a mini flash-back of the Dutch coffee shop clerk smiling, 'and please don't mix these shrooms, ja. It could be very intense you understand. Take at your own risk. Good luck.'

'You still fucked?'

I shrug, 'yeah a little I guess. Shit's still moving around but nothing compared to the last few hours. How long do you think the whole trip lasted, you know how they say time distorts an all?'

'Shit, I don't know siss, I didn't exactly keep track if you know what I mean.'

At that moment, Kay stirs on the other side of the bed. She is faced away but at least tries to join the conversation.

Kay imitates Joey from *Friends,* 'how you doin Lo?'

'Still with us are we? I'm cool now, but my head was sure fucked up for a while there. Wasn't sure if I was ever coming back, you know what I mean?'

'I wish I could have been there with you, maybe I could have helped.' Kay proving she was genuinely concerned for me.

'You couldn't have. I mean no one would have wanted to be where I was. I was all alone with no one to help me but myself. I never really knew what it was like to be truly *stuck* before. Now I do.'

'Oh, I'm sorry to hear that. Well as long as you're OK now, that's what matters. You're back.'

I look over to see if she'll make some kind of eye contact with me, but she remains hidden under the covers as if embarrassed that she is naked in front of me.

I have a small tear in my eye, 'your right siss, but I wasn't even in the same dimension as you guys. I mean my body was still on the couch downstairs, but in my mind I was off miles away. I even saw the world from space.'

J chips in again finally, 'that's cool, I had a space trip once.'

Deadly serious, 'yeah? But I bet yours didn't have the world blowing up did it?'

J opens his eyes, and sits up. 'You serious? No wonder you were havin a bad one, you saw the end of the world yo.'

'Nahhhh! You reckon? I dunno bro; I haven't put all the pieces together yet. I couldn't figure it all out . . . yet.'

'You will, with time. It doesn't always happen overnight, you know?

I continue rationalising, 'yeah but this trip really was different man. I mean it really was new, you know? I had a full body trip, not just hallucinations, but the works.'

Kay sits up properly keeping her bits covered, 'Lo you sure you're OK?'

'I'm fine …. I think. I think I might have had a vision or a . . . what's it called? Oh yeah like an epiphany or something.'

'Slow down there partner. You don't fully know what you saw and why.'

J being a hippy, 'why's everything gotta mean something? Couldn't we just chillax and have some fun here. You guys are getting too deep.'

I take a few more drags on the spliff, 'I have to figure this out somehow. Maybe not tonight, but I will sooner or later. I must.'

'Look Lo, slow down OK. Finish the joint and maybe go lie down and rest. You still haven't slept that much remember?'

'I know, don't worry about me. You guys go back to sleep, I can't go back to dream world yet. I need to kill some time.'

'K, but try not to make too much noise alright?'

'I gotcha. Cheers for listening you two, the others just passed out on me.'

My brother, relaxed as ever, 'it's OK Lo, try and get some rest.'

I politely excuse myself and head back downstairs, find my camera and go to the far end of the house to whisper quietly for my video diary. I fiddle with the camera switching it on, opening the LCD screen flipping it so I can see myself in shot. I've never really done one of these before but somehow I think it should be on record. I finally press the red button.

'This is Lorraine Kingston reporting live (giggling still *coming down*) from a house in middle of fucking nowhere. In the flattest part of Holland you could imagine. I have just come out of the most intense trip of my life and survived it. Afterwards I saw something strange when I was outta the trip. One of the guys here he had (pause) black eyes. Not quite sure what it means yet. I'm guessing something psychological…'

I hear random applause in my head as I continue to document my *story*. I do this mainly since I have no one else to talk to and have never done a video diary before in my life, but now seems like the best time ever. Plus the experience is still fresh in my mind and I want to document it like a will of sorts. The number 2012 sticks in my mind for some reason, I don't mention it at the time. Maybe it was something to do with the timecode….

The New Year's trip has come to an end, back to reality and getting back to the world. The five members of our journey look dishevelled and are waiting by the train tracks, eagerly expecting the train that is taking a while. J and I walk off down the track to smoke one of the last joints we have before heading back to London via Amsterdam. Everyone else passed on the spliff so it's up the two hard-core party siblings to say our goodbyes to the countryside.

I take a toke off the joint, 'well, Holland. I guess that's a trip I won't ever forget for like the rest of my life.'

J turns towards the countryside. 'Amen to that. I would like to say it has been my pleasure tripping in your presence. Till we meet again?'

'You think we'll ever come back here again, bro?'

'I dunno. That's up to the fates to decide.'

I'm intrigued by this last comment, 'the fates huh? I always thought there was only one.'

Honestly, he says, 'I just made that up. Plus I'm still come down from the last couple days.'

'No, it's cool. It's a nice way to finish. To the fates then.' I offer up the joint to the world.

'Sweet, don't wear it out,' J finishes the joint and stubs it out. Him coughing we walk back to the others as our train arrives on the platform.

CHAPTER 9 – BACK AGAIN

J, Kay, and I have arrived back at our flat. China and Jack aren't with us anymore since they don't live together. After putting our bags down, J and I sit down to have a welcome back bong. After packing it and taking a hit he passes it to me, cautious at first but then I take a pretty big hit. Kay plays some music on the stereo Type-O-Negative's *Green Man* track.

'So, we're finally back, eh?'

J nods, 'yeah I guess. It's weird being back after such a trip.'

'Same. I think I gotta figure out what exactly I saw. I'm gonna read up about trips and visions.'

J offers his corner of random books on a shelf, 'be my guest I don't really have anything here, but I'm sure you can find out about that stuff online or at the library.'

Whilst checking out the selection, I look back at him curiously, 'you reckon they'll have books on that shit do ya?'

'Sure they do, you just gotta know where to look. I think you'll be wasting your time though.'

'How you figure?'

'It's all just your mind fucking with ya' J assertively.

'I disagree, I think I've been shown something special on purpose and I'm meant to get to the bottom of it.' I'm adamant.

'It's your funeral. Ha ha. Tripping is just fun, that's all it is yo. Don't think about it too much, it'll drive you crazy.'

I reminisce, 'well I don't care about that. I don't believe it's just bull shit you know? Remember Amsterdam that first time?'

'Sure I do, it was cool at the time, but that's all it is. End of story.' J packs another bong and hits it.

'You seriously don't think there's more to it than that? I see that time as the beginning of my inner journey.'

'Call it what you like, I've pretty much forgotten most it already.'

'That sucks bro. I did a video diary and wrote it down. One day I'm gonna write a book then a screenplay on it. I'm not gonna just forget it like you did.'

'I'm just saying be careful, OK? The subconscious can really do a number on some people.'

I continue, 'yeah, regarding that. I told you Jack had black eyes when I came out of the trip didn't I?'

'That means you were still trippin obviously Lo.'

'It was more than that. I didn't have any other hallucinations after I came out of that trip. I think there is a deeper meaning to what I saw OK.'

'Whatever,' my brother bringing back that evil word from the first Dam trip.

'That's what I kept on saying after that first trip in Dam!'

'Yeah? You know what I say to that? Whatever!'

I try to bring warmth back into the room, 'that's pretty cold bro. Maybe we should stop talking about it.'

He snorts - 'fine.'

I give J a strange look, as if I don't remember my brother anymore. It's as if through that conversation I lost all respect for his spirituality. We sit in silence, while Kay is going in and out of the rooms, unpacking, getting herself together, etc.

I'm at the library surfing the web going through loads of conspiracy web sites regarding end of the world scenarios. I come across Graham Hancock's *Fingerprints of the Gods* and even start researching the number 2012. I also find a book online by Daniel Pinchbeck *2012: The Return of Quetzalcoatl*. I read blogs on various web sites, including stuff on aliens, HAARP project, and ancient South American and Egyptian history/mythology. I'm really into this stuff now, I'm more passionate about this research then when I was studying at school. I take loads of notes during this process, looking around every now and then to make sure no one is looking. Just in case someone thinks I'm a conspiracy freak or somethin. The other *surfers* are mostly checking emails or playing some computer games with headphones on. I pack away my notes and grab my bag after the pre-pay time runs out.

I continue my research at the library going through the catalogues, even asking the librarian for help/info from time to time.

'So, sorry to bother again but I was wondering if you could help me track down some books I can't find. I got this one (holding up *Fingerprints of the Gods*), but I still can't track down this 2012 book I found online.'

The librarian is pleasantly patient with me despite my excess energy. 'OK, hang on a second let me bring it up and see if I can find it.'

I hand her a note with the info: Daniel Pinchbeck's *2012: The Return of Quetzalcoatl*. She runs it through the computer database.

'Ah yes, here it is. Oh I'm sorry, we don't stock it here, since it's an American author who hasn't sold many copies over here, so unfortunately we don't have it, but I'm sure you could order it from a local book store.'

She hands me back the piece of paper. 'Sorry darling, good luck with your search through.'

'OK, forget it. I'll just check out these ones for now then I guess.' I hand her Graham Hancock's *Fingerprints of the Gods* and a couple others, including the two *Bible Code* books.

'Sure, can I see your membership card?'

'Um, I don't have one yet. Sorry.'

'How about some ID then?'

I dig around in my wallet and find it eventually. A small queue has built up behind me at this stage. I look behind me sheepishly, I grin as a couple shuffle their feet. Excited, I'm confident that very soon I can begin my mission of explanations and theories.

That night I sit by myself in the TV room, I'm reading and taking notes on the first couple books, which are littered with post-its on several pages. A bong is sitting on the table in front of me, leaking out smoke from the top of the chamber. Of course I'm still gonna partake. A cloud of smoke sits in the air only being moved around when I lean forward to write down some notes from time to time. Heh, I didn't say anything about quitting weed just gonna take a break from tripping for a while and learn more about the *bad one*.

Whilst studying, flashbacks of the previous times tripping with my brother and on my own including the *bad trip night* pass through my mind. Intertwined with new information of ancient Egyptians, South American Mayans and Aztecs studying the skies and constellations. I flip between the texts, reading sporadically. In my head I hear stuff J said about it all being fake and that *trips* didn't mean anything. I look up every now and then as if contemplating what I'm researching, and then I continue taking some more notes. I even start to type some info out on my lap top, which rests beside me the whole time.

J and Kay come in the room tipsy from a night of partying. This disturbance of my peace puts me off from my studies. I'm slightly upset since I was really getting into the research, I pack my lap top and notes away as Kay sits down next to me, to have some *girly* chat.

'So what you been up to today Lo?'

'I've been doing some homework.'

Kay smiling tipsily, 'for school? I thought you haven't started yet?'

'Yeah, I mean no I haven't. I've been doing some reading up about 2012, the end of the world and confirmed visions by shamans and some conspiracy theorists.'

'Wow, slow down. Just remember not to totally believe everything you read, OK?' Slurring her words and blinking slowly as drunk people do.

'Of course, I gotta take this stuff with a pinch of salt. It's just I really wanna understand what happened that night on New Year's, you know?'

'That's all well and good Lo, just don't get bogged down with this stuff that's all. How long you been "studying" then?' Kay picks up one of my books and flips through the pages quickly looking for some interesting pictures. Finding some on ancient astronauts and murals with alien-like creatures on some of the pages.

I think for a second, 'since . . . all day I think.'

Surprised, 'all day! Wow, you really are serious about this shit aren't cha?'

'Hell yeah. Of course, what's wrong with a bit of research, huh?'

'Yeah I suppose. Heh, I support you, just put it away and have a drink with me, OK?' Kay gives me a kiss on my forehead as she wraps her arm around my neck. J comes in at that moment with some Coronas/Sols, and 3 shot glasses. He places them on the table and grabs a half empty bottle of Tequila from the cabinet. He pours the glasses, when Kay jumps up and goes into the kitchen. J and I give each other a funny look as she didn't say why she got up so suddenly.

'You OK hon?'

Kay still rustling in the kitchen. 'Yeah hold on, I'm just getting somethin.'

'Yeah OK, hurry up though I wanna do these,' J drooling over the shots.

Kay comes half-skipping back into the room excited like a kid. She has a small bottle of Tabasco sauce and half a lime.

'Sorry guys. You reminded me, I just had to try these with you since some American guys ordered it at the bar tonight.' Kay takes the bottle shakes a couple drops into each shot glass, and then squeezes the lime into all three. She holds hers up, I stand up at this point and we all clink our glasses together.

All in unison, 'cheers! Bottoms up!'

We all do the shots, licking our lips directly after the shock from the harshness of the tequila. Kay and I laugh as we all look a little blown away by the power of the shots.

'Wow, that's pretty fucking awesome yo.'

'See, I told ya. The guys were just having the shots with the Tequila and Tabasco, but it was my idea to squirt the lime into them.'

'Fuckin sweeeeeet!!!!'

Bowing I say, 'I take my hat off to ya, that shit really is good. It takes off the edge of the tequila by balancing it with the spicy flavour.'

'I know. It's like they were made for each other and no one has ever really done it. I mean they're from the same part of the world, right? So they're made for each other, huh?'

'Definitely. Let's have another one.' We cheer as Kay and J get even drunker. I simply try to catch up, so I chug my beer to top myself up. The night continues with more shots, bongs, a couple joints, even Kay has a couple tokes despite the fact that she normally doesn't smoke. Red-eyed we party till the morning hours.

CHAPTER 10 – COPS

BANG-BANG-BANG!!!!

I don't know what's going on, am I still dreaming. Loud sounds fluctuate in and out of my mind then I snap awake realizing it's not a dream. Someone is at the door shouting and banging hard. I call out to my bro.

'J! J! Someones at the door!'

I start getting dressed as I take a peek out the window I see a riot van parked outside on the street. A couple cops are on the sidewalk ushering people along their way.

'Cops! Fucking cops are here!' At that moment J comes storming down the stairs half-dressed trying to get his T-shirt on. He joins me by the window and looks out baffled. That can't be for us we think in unison.

'This is the police! Open this door immediately or we will be forced to break it down!

J and I look at each other in disbelief. What the fuck did we do to warrant this abuse? We quickly look around to see if any drugs and/or paraphernalia are cluttered around the house in view. We hide one of the bongs and our drug tin first, J forgets about some speed hidden away in a drawer with various letters.

'We gotta open the door,' he directs at me. I see no out either. We mentally agree it's that or worst case scenario, they bust down the down the door and we still get busted anyway. J goes to the front door and lets the nightmare in.

'Stand back you! Hands on your 'ed mate! Turn around and face the wall!' They seem to storm in by the dozens, we are treated like proper criminals, let alone terrorists. They cuff J first even though we haven't been read our rights or told what we did to deserve this. They see me and come after me next literally forcing me to the couch to stay seated after they cuff me behind the back. J is lead back into our main den, our soon to be ex-favourite room of the apartment. They sit him down next to me also cuffed behind the back.

There isn't much space around so they seem to move in a single file. Like robots or ants on the march they start searching around immediately while one main officer addresses us. 'Are you Mr. Jay Smith, renter of this apartment?'

'What's this all about?' My brother enquires before he is shut down quickly.

'I'll be asking the questions around here son.'

'Yes, that's me,' he reluctantly gives up with his head bowed.

'We have suspicion to believe you are a major drug supplier in the area, are there any drugs on the premises?' This cop is so by the book he literally has it shoved up his ass 24/7.

J and I look at each other embarrassed and still in shock at the situation. A couple seconds go by with our thoughts a mess. I keep thinking is this a flash back to that first night on New Year's in Holland. This is more realistic than any dream or trip I've ever had, I'm hung over, tired as hell and groggy to boot. This can't be happening but it is.

'Well? I asked you a question boy,' the officer stares down on at us as if a giant looming over its prey. I have a flash of fear and paranoia as it reminds me of my second night on New Year's. The soldier shadow creature.

My bro defiant as ever stares up at him in racist disbelief, 'what did you just call me?'

The cop doesn't like that attitude one bit so he bends down sharply and gets real close to my bro's face, nearly nose to nose. Other constables edge closer in case things get out of hand and they have to restrain me and/or J, not to protect their superintendent. 'Listen here you. We are police enforcers of the law via her majesties service and we are here to do our job. Make it easier on yourself and tell us where your stash is, we know you're a dealer mate.'

'Stash? Dealer? Where do you guys get your intel from?'

Officer dick-head goes red in the face and stands up

straight as if about to hit J in the face. He holds back as there is a gasp from the other pigs in the room.

I like bacon but most people my age don't like cops or the institutions they *protect and serve*. Kay is brought down to our fray as well now yet they didn't cuff her for some reason, a cop just holds her by her arm so she can't struggle. Confusion and tears are visible on her face. Us criminals, are still bound to our seat mentally as well as physically.

'I'll ask you one last time.' He has actually relaxed a little and has a breather facing away from us.

My brother finally relinquishes, 'fine I'll tell you. The sooner we can get this over with.'

'He joins us on planet earth at last' - the cop snorts vindictively.

Ignoring this comment J spills the goods, just not the goods they wanna hear, 'there's a bong over there in the corner. Some hash in a tin in that drawer and roach butts all over the place.' All he can do is nod in the directions mentioned since he can't point anywhere.

PC dickhead orders his minions around into the exact locations described, looks like at first they didn't find what they were looking for so they bring out all the *evidence* and lay it all out on our table in front of us. No magic trick here only harsh cold reality. Luckily, it's not very much to go by since we partied hard last night. The room still has the faint smell of smoke and spilled beer lingering.

You can tell the cops are disgusted by the hygiene of the place. A female officer attempts to open the blinds, but the handle is broken so it all collapses in front of her leaving a trace of dust floating through the room picking up early morning rays of sunshine coming through the windows. She walks away like it wasn't her fault. My bro and I chuckle since we don't find it that gross I mean we do clean once every couple months or so.

'Shut up!' Dickhead snaps. He does not excuse our behaviour one bit and slowly it's dawning on him that this bust is not the career promotion he was hoping for. The cops go through the house and in the end they just dump all the ashtrays they can find onto the table. Not placing them properly but leaving the mess and the stink ruining the mood even more. 'Where's the rest of it? Are you telling me you're not this dealer we are led to believe?'

'What can I say doc? I'm just a simple stoner trying to make it in the world,' cool as ever he replies.

'And you, what about you um Miss or are you a man? I can't even tell with that rag on your head.' He and the others have a good chuckle over this as if my dreads didn't take hard work maintaining and years of not washing.

I don't find this amusing and my snappy side gets me into trouble again. 'Oh yeah? And why did you suspect my brother in the first place huh? It's cause he's mixed race right? He's not even full black you racist fucks!' Even my bro is surprised by my answer, feeling the love and respect we shared over the past year.

'How dare you! You cheeky git! Don't you know what country you're in? You bloody yank!'

'We're actually half English if you did your homework copper,' my bro tries to take the heat off me.

'I don't give a toss where you're from! I'm the law here and you're not so special cause you're from yankee land!' He stands proud with his hands on his hips thinking he's a superhero or something.

Kay continues sobbing slouched down on the floor as the cop tries to pin her down holding onto her shoulder. This insult to our international upbringing stings a sore wound since we never had a choice in moving around the world. We didn't choose to have an American accent it just developed for most of us *ex-pats* (ex-patriots).

'Look that's it OK, so what's next here man?' My bro cuts through the red tape and gets to the point.

Officer Dickhead admits defeat and orders the team to bag and tag the room. 'Alright everyone bag the evidence and let's head back to the station, this wasn't the bust we had hoped for, just some bad intel. We'll issue a warning to the neighbours regarding false accusations in the future.'

It's as if we ruined their morning, you could hear it in his voice, he wasn't happy with his bust. We were a disappointment to him even. It's seven AM now, we only just got to bed at five. Two hours sleep and he's pissed, I was still wasted even now.

'Lead em out. We're done here. Leave the girlfriend behind. She is innocent in this matter.' He gives her a sleazy look as he leaves the room.

We are led down past more cops waiting in the stair way, one is even holding a battering ram to the side. I can't believe they would have broken down J's door, for what? Cannabis sativa, enemy number one. The curse of the world. OMG. Is the world and the rules retarded or is it just me?

I jog down the stairs like I always do and instantly behind me I hear a 'HALT! Stand still and wait!' I freeze like a statue interrupted in my *stair routine*. As if I'm gonna run off with cuffs behind my back. Really? Sunshine blinds me as I exit the building, my retinas hurt momentarily as they adjust to the sudden light change. The cop behind me leads me on towards the back of the riot van. Before we enter J and I notice the gay neighbours standing on the other side of the road holding each other in fear of the situation. How did they ever end up living next to two of the biggest druggies (not dealers) in London. Oh my, the gossip. My bro and I give them the evils knowing they were the ones that have done this to us. They think they are clever hiding behind all the police and cars, but we know the truth. The back of the van has chains interlinking handcuffs that we are connected to. They strap us in and leave us in the back as they shut the doors. What? No supervision? After all that we could be escape artists since we were already treated like professional criminals i.e. terrorists.

Once at the station we are taken through the mundane task of finger printing and every possible detail is taken down including any piercings and birth mark(s). This is before the days of compulsory DNA swabs but still it is so degrading to be going through this procedure of becoming a database criminal. No matter what happens in the future I will have my record with prints and all locked away in a computer folder for all eternity. When they say your record gets wiped after a few years, its hogwash. It's for life my friends. You think if you become a real terrorist one day they just say oops we lost your file, they have your *jacket* for as long as they want it just depends on your security clearance to access it. After all the photos and boring stuff they locked me in a cell by myself. To pass the time I did some push ups went to the toilet (all in one small room) and laid down for a bit on the bunk but no sleep returned. This was too crazy and surreal a place. Every now and then the hatch would open and a couple of eyes would appear to check to see if I was still alive I guess. Every time I sat up as if to be lead out of this bad dream but as soon as I was about to speak it shut instantly leaving me with a half open mouth probably looking pretty sheepish. A couple hours pass and it's time to go. My bro and I are kept separate but they let me out first back into the reception/booking area.

One of the officers at our crime scene sits me down and gives me a lecture I will never forget. 'You know smoking Cannabis is very bad for your health, you're much better off drinking I reckon.'

'You mean like alcohol? I do that too, but I will never be an alcoholic. There's too much of that in my family already.'

'I'm not saying be an alcoholic, but the truth of the matter is that cannabis is illegal in this country and we police the rules, you see?' He is quite pleased with himself thinking he is doing God's work here; he probably goes to church as so many Brits do.

'Thanks for the lecture but you are aware that weed can

cure cancer right?' I bust out some of my permanent info regarding one of my most knowledgeable subjects.

'Bollocks! Where'd you get that intel from mate?' He squints at me as I de-rail him from his job duties.

'It's fact, in the 70's a European Doctor in America treated and cured thousands of patients. The FDA took him to court trying to sue him for the formula but he wouldn't budge and they never managed to prosecute him. Fact mate.' Don't know why I'm so cranky all of a sudden, oh yeah it's because my whole day has been ruined.

'Oh, I get it. You're one of those conspiracy nuts innit?' He leans back yet frustrated that I'm listening to his words and still choosing to ignore his advice.

'And don't get me started on booze,' I continue, 'thousands of years and still no one has a cure for hang overs. Can you explain that?' I have a moment of relief getting my info out to the man with the uniform, but am quickly shut down again.

'Listen here, I'm telling you what's good for you. Don't try and turn this around on me you hear.' He's having none of it and looks at his watch in an excuse to get away from me.

I try even harder thinking I might get through to him still, 'and hemp has been used for hundreds of years as rope, paper and even medicine. Can you say the same of al-co-hol?'

'Enough chit chat young lady, you need to sign some discharge papers then you may leave.' He stands up and leads me back to the *receptionist* and drops me off without a goodbye.

He has already turned away as I have one last stab virtually all in one breath, 'and the American declaration of independence and the first dollar bills were printed with hemp. Proven to be a hundred times more productive than regular paper which is used by cutting down rainforests destroying species and medicines yet to be discovered!' I inhale deeply.

'Bugger off!' He mumbles under his breath as he exits back to his desk job and what I consider the most redundant job in the world.

I shake my head unable to reason with *these people*.

'Oi, sign here!' Are the last words spoken to me in my *confinement*.

CHAPTER 11 – AFTERMATH

That night, arguments increase in the house. We come back to a different home, one with no smoke and now one less bong. How dare we, how dare they! We all drink since nothing else is available to us now. J flips out every now and then, Kay cries at times. I try to defend her but J starts shouting at me too. Separately everyone takes turns sulking on the couch at different times. The fights are usually pointless, due to J's on-going depression and *rage attacks*. When we are alone together, J touches a nerve when he gives me grief for believing in all *the spiritual bullshit* then I retaliate with J not being *spiritual* anymore. He in return says it's all for nothing.

J ranting at me, 'I had to go to church daily remember in boarding school, what did you ever do?'

I react, 'don't use that against me, you know I never wanted either of us to go to boarding school. It was Dad all along. You had to go first cause you were older!'

'Fuck that! I was sent cause I was the odd one out of the family. You all were white, and I'm half-caste!'

'I don't care about any of that! You should know by now you're the only brother I've ever had! You are my family over here.'

'Oh yeah, well maybe you should go back Stateside and leave me the fuck alone!'

'Fuck bro. What's up with you? You depressed again or something? I thought you don't get like this anymore.'

'Whatever! Fuck you! You guys were never my family; I made it on my own. Without any of your help.'

'J! Sorry, I don't know what to say. What can I do? It's not my fault it panned out the way it did. I offered you to go to Dad's funeral remember, you had a chance to be a part of our family and you pissed all over our offer.'

'I couldn't care less about Dad after he left us.'

'And what about Mom, she was there for us, and now you guys don't even talk with each other anymore.'

'I don't need her and I don't need you!'

'That hurts man. Is that it then? Whatever happened to our blood oath?'

J looks a little upset by this; I finally got through to him somewhere.

'It didn't mean anything; I was wasted at the time.'

Now I'm offended properly, 'oh yeah? And I suppose our trips together means fuck all to you too huh?'

J goes over to a corner and has his back towards me, even though he has quieted down now.

'Whatever!' He mumbles.

I'm crying too now, Kay has left the room crying on her own upstairs.

'Well it does to me. It was so great to hang out with you again, after so many years apart.'

J is silent now, but he lights up a cigarette and takes deep drags still turned away from me.

J's tone changes quiet after the storm, 'maybe it's my brain surgery still why I get these outbreaks.'

'That's well and good, but don't forget who your real family is. Don't forget about me and Kay alright. Or do all the times we've spent with you mean nothing?'

'I dunno, maybe. I mean yes . . . and no.'

I feel snubbed, 'you don't mean that.'

'What if I do? What you gonna do about it?' J snaps.

'Nothing I guess, I'm hoping you'll phase out of this ... whatever it is. Look, I'm onto something here. The pieces of the puzzle are finally falling into place. I see similarities with you now and what I used to be like when I was younger. I would have fits of anger too, but I've managed to control them over the years. Bro you know I'm chilled and I would never hurt you.'

He continues, 'yeah well you didn't go through what I did with my surgery, did you?'

'Of course not, but this isn't how it has to end.'

J turns around and looks me in the eyes; he is hiding a couple of tears too now. Instead of walking up to me and hugging me, he simply walks by and goes upstairs to his bedroom, not saying anything. I'm left by myself, sitting alone in the now quiet TV/living room. I sit motionless as my eyes glide around the room, looking at a broken spare bong. Our ashtrays with ciggie butts and joint roaches still piled up on top of the table. Empty beer cans are strewn around the floor and table. I sigh several times, wiping away the last of my tears. I'm still in shock at what just happened. How could we have gone from loving siblings until that New Year's night, when everything seemed to change for me, and maybe even my brother also? I get up and start packing some of my things, I do it slowly though, hoping J will come down and apologize and everything will be OK again, but he doesn't. I never see him again. I leave them a note and after a phone call to the airline I head to the airport.

I guess there is no fixing this; all I can do now is figure out what caused all this mess. If I never mentioned my trip would this still have panned out the way it did? I want to change my life, maybe I'll become a Buddhist or something. First things first.

CHAPTER 12 – FINALE

I arrive back home and spot my Mom waving eagerly, I grin out of embarrassment, but am glad to be on American soil again. Some of my dreads have come out having formed into spirals like Angelina Jolie in *Gone in 60 Seconds*. I had to quit film school and leave London behind. I have a new beginning now away from my brother, and sadly leaving Kay behind as well. I felt like the three of us were inseparable, until that fateful day of my brother's final stand. I'm jet lagged and still confused about what happened back in the London flat. My Mom grabs me and squeezes me tight, even though I barely lift a hand. Instead I just look over her shoulder at all the other families re-united and overly happy.

'Oh baby, it's so good to have you home again. I'm so sorry to hear what happened to you and J. Now you see why we've had difficulty getting along with him over the years. He still holds a grudge against us for what happened all those years ago.'

I forgive her instantly happy to be in her arms again, 'it's OK Mom, I'm back now. But not for long, I have to re-apply to film school over here ASAP.'

'Well I hope it's close so we can still visit each other.'

'I hate to break it to you, but I was thinking the coast. I wanna be by the ocean again.'

Mom surprised, 'the ocean! You sure that's what you want?'

Mom has already taken my bag off me as we walk through the terminal and head for the exit.

'I haven't decided which side yet. Either Cali or Miami. I need some coastal sun after my stay in London.'

'If that's what you want. We still have lots of sun here in Arizona.'

I give her a questioning look of disapproval. 'I still wanna be by the ocean Mom. Or travel somewhere.'

'OK darling, whatever you think is right. I love you no matter what, you know that don't you?'

Arm in arm walking out the terminal towards her car. 'Yeah I know. I'm cool though, you don't have to worry about me, I can take care of myself now.'

'Yeah I noticed.' Mom struggles with my bag as we exit the building.

Years pass as I wait for the fateful date of 21st of December 2012, the end of the Mayan calendar. Will it be the end of the world as I saw in my trip or will nothing happen at all? I think about the millennium bug theories returning, all technology being wiped out by an EMP. Anything is possible, surely a revolution or something. C'mon I mean something has gotta happen right? The second coming of Christ perhaps. An alien invasion? Armageddon.

I'm on a Californian beach listening to my MP3 player and one of my favourite songs ever *Ashes to Ashes* by Faith no More is playing in my headphones. Hearing the lyrics *Smiling with my Mouth to the Ocean* I become emotional even since I'm sitting alone on the beach. Waves splashing on the shore, I can hear sounds of seagulls as they fly around me. My hair flows loosely in the wind as I have my pony-tail undone. I'm crying as my eyes drift along the horizon. I look down to the sand; I forgot I'm holding a gun. It is a lightweight and highly accurate Glock pistol. I have it in my palm facing sideways keeping it as a safety net in case a huge tidal wave heads towards me. My brother said he had night terrors for years where he'd be sitting in his room and a gigantic inescapable tidal wave was heading towards him. That always stuck in my mind especially since the recent devastating Tsunamis around the globe. Climate change, global warming has come and it's here to stay. For now this peaceful beach is where I want to be at this moment.

Well how to finish such a tale, that's a tricky one. As you gathered, I moved away from London, my brother, and after a short stint at home I moved to the coast and started my new life. I began film school properly this time and guess what? Over the years I continued researching spiritualism and hallucinogens. I even went down to South America via Mexico and tripped with Shamans. Ayuahuasca, peyote, shrooms whatever the locals were doing. Daniel Pinchbeck's *2012* book was a big inspiration to me and I asked many of the same questions he did. What will happen on or after the 21st of December 2012? No one seemed to have an answer. Simply put, they could not see beyond that date, which didn't help my on-off paranoia. I practiced Shamanism for a while, something that always intrigued me. I stayed with tribes of the Amazonian rain forest and even tried the hallucinogenic frog poison for a change. What did all this do for me you ask?

I'll never forget the times that I had, the stuff I saw. In the end it took me a couple years to really get to grips with happened to me, and my subconscious, that New Year's. I don't regret it because it showed me what extent the mind can go to at times. See, I was always looking for answers in my trips. Not even asking the questions going into them, but deep down my brain was trying to figure out the truth all the time. Why are we here? What purpose do we have in life? More specifically, what are de-ja-vu and dreams? And what happens in the afterlife, i.e. death? Well the first time I took copious amounts of shrooms I found out the answer to the first question. The next time I did that much, probably even more (since we mixed more than we should have) I was shown a possible outcome of our *human race*. Don't get me wrong, I sure as hell don't want the world to end today on the 21st of December, 2012. But at the same time there's not a day that went by in the last twelve years I didn't think about it.

I'll be here all day waiting if I have to . . . *smiling with my mouth to the ocean.*

AFTERWORD

As I said in the foreword most of the tripping stories told in this book really happened. The family tales were mainly fictional; to create the tension/depression I was feeling inside when I was younger. Taking drugs helped me grow to the point where I didn't want to accept the fact of death as part of life. I put it out of my mind until my bad trip experience where I could no longer avoid the question: what happens when we die? My father believes that's it, the end; others believe in a heaven and hell scenario. I was shown purgatory. It was nothing like I would have imagined.

The worst part was that it was so real, the torment I went through with various mental, visual and even *physical* changes during the trip. Towards the end when the visuals were dying down I felt like the release (with the help of my bro's coconut bong) was finally down to state of mind. Having been in that world for hours (which felt like eternity) I resolved that I was done for. Like a DMT experience you die and come out on the other side reborn/fresh. Coming out of the most intense hallucination of my life I was happier than ever, telling everyone I could about the experience having more fun talking about it than being in it. It took me a few years to truly understand what it meant.

Over the years I really believed it was a sign and I was chosen. I told everyone about the Mayan calendar ending and of a possible end of world scenario. Don't misunderstand me, I was not ranting on a street corner but brought it up in casual conversation to see if anyone else was like me out there. Before and after 2012 I have met many people like me that believed the end was coming. Personally I was in Portugal hiking in the mountains visiting an ancient Moorish/Templar fort expecting a giant tidal wave. My brother and others used to have end of the world dreams including this very common tidal wave outside a house type scenario. I would only ever have zombie apocalypse dreams, never ones of that kind.

Yet through my Erik Van Daniken and other 2012 books I was heavily influenced into believing something was coming or going to happen. Obviously nothing happened yet many of us talked about a spiritual shift due to take place. Many shamans could not see past that 21st of December date, which made me even more paranoid when I thought about that fateful day.

This book is an external representation of what I believed in and trips that changed me over the years. Not all are documented in this book since I wanted to focus on the magic mushrooms in particular. Taking Acid for many years prior to my Holland experiences I never encountered anything on the level of the intensity of those trips. My only regret is not mentioning my Peyote experience in Mexico, which in a way pre-empted my bad trip before my death trip. I saw many demons and skulls in the sky formed by the clouds yet remained unaffected by this *message* until the sky cleared and a guardian angel flew down and all the bad elements disappeared in the process. It seemed I was protected and I felt this till the day where I was all alone in my full 360 vision of purgatory where my guardian angel was nowhere to be seen. I was truly alone in the world at that time.

I hope this book has given you an insight to how tripping can be dangerous and spiritual at the same time. Despite the bad energy created I feel like I have grown more than ever writing this down and letting the world read about me and my experiences. Hope you take something with you from this life.

ENERGY

Before I ever read or heard of the book "Discover your psychic powers: A practical guide to Psychic Development & Spiritual Growth" By Tara Ward I experienced/ witnessed Cosmic/Earth Energy at 1) the eclipse festival in Cornwall (2000) or at 2) Glastonbury Music Festival (2000).

Eclipse festival:

Firstly, I took a tab of acid mixing with E's (Mitsubishis). This union can prove treacherous at times, but in this instance it was the perfect combination; which helped me have the double hallucinatory/wavy effect needed to see waves of energy floating in the sky above us. Sometimes part of the clouds other times in front of it, as if weaving in and out an invisible wall yet from my point of view was similar to a hologram. Since this was my first time tripping after my bad trip I was cautious at first, but once I saw this I wanted to learn more or at least understand what I saw exactly. Since I was coming down I wanted to prolong the experience so I opened up my eyes wider, feeling slightly awkward since I was letting more light then usual into my retinas, however it slightly extended my power to witness energy.

    I've only been convinced of auras once when I was out in Palenque (Mexico), when we were hanging out with some Mexican dudes and one of them said in response to seeing me and my brother's girlfriend together, that we had good/great auras, we thanked him and he continued his conversation with a friend as if it was completely normal for him. I remember feeling really good about myself and the world since I always preferred this spirituality opposed to conventional religions. I always wondered what my aura would look like now, since this was before my bad trip experience.

In her book Tara Ward talks about the 7 levels of auras surrounding each person: Divine mind, divine love, divine will, relationships with others, rational mind, emotions with respect to self, and physical sensation. She says that if specific issues are not dealt with accordingly, there are blockages within individual auras, which upsets the balance of the whole system. As I was reading about each level, part of me was like "fuck this shit" explaining why my subconscious was still trying to deal with the two bad trip experiences I thought I was over with. On the other hand she spoke of a spiritual truth I was still learning about and coming to understand.

That's why I stopped tripping cause I think I don't have the power to deal with those situations anymore since second time round (on New Year's) it occurred was even more frightening on a visual/sensual level. I was actually trying to force my hallucinations to stop instead of trying to deal with the age old issue: that we all die someday and am convinced there is an afterlife. Through certain unusual emotions and stories, part of me still fears death like all others. Once the hallucinations stopped I was back in reality and was given a second chance to change my life.

It took me a few years until I read 'Fingerprints of the Gods' by Graham Hancock and realized I feared the end of all our existence in 2012. So I lived life fearing that day not just for me, but for all of us. I wouldn't be upset about the shattering of industry and technology, but the destruction of mother earth on a cosmic level. Some scientists reckoned our polar caps were going to switch like in the ice age (every 10,000 years) but what if all our evolution/technology failed on that day (or following days) and we were back at ground zero with no electricity and no power to save ourselves. What then?

Glastonbury:

Anyways, my second experience was a bit smaller, but nevertheless a reminder that certain areas on the earth have energy fields across the globe (Leylines). I'm not sure if Cornwall has any passing through, but I know for certain that Glastonbury does (common pagan knowledge) and after taking a hit of Acid (cinnamon flavored) I was walking around with my friends, not hallucinating yet feeling that 'acid high' as if severely/pleasantly high.

Some lady offered us 'energy balls' at first I declined, but then thought what the hell, they were only a pound each. At first it tasted strange like healthy protein cookies but in a solid ball shape. They weren't tiny either, they would fit perfectly in your mouth and once I chewed it I knew they were something special. I almost immediately noticed it traveling slowly through my body warming up my esophagus and into my intestines to be digested where it sat glowing until I was unaware of the sensation anymore. As we strolled around I started to notice circles of energy on the side of our path, I told my hippie friends what I was seeing, but they seemed unaffected by my telling them that I could see energy, not like I had before (covering the whole sky above me for the Eclipse festival).

In the best way to describe it is outside Dracula's castle in Francis Ford Coppola' reworking of Bram Stoker's classic novella by the scene where Dracula's spirit possesses Winona Ryder's character and Van Helsing has to witness the brides of Dracula stab his horse to death. There is a visual (CG) FX shot where outside his big gates there are blue circular flames motioning upwards in a tubular shape, but consistent. If you don't know which scene I'm talking about, I recommend trying to find it on your Blu-Ray/DVD cause it's hard to imagine if you don't understand what they might be.

I think they are little pockets of energy leading upwards connecting the ground with the sky. Granted, I could only see human height ones before they disappeared, they didn't reach all the way up into the sky. So maybe they are related to the height of our auras all mingling together. Or maybe they are just springs releasing energy from the ground into the air. I'm just telling you what I saw and what these 'visions' mean to me. If you do know please try and contact me, since I am still not all *knowledgeable*. I just don't have the same drive and curiosity as I used to, I feel I know more than I did then looking back only wishing I could return to those states.

Certain people can tap into it automatically or with meditation, but I always feel we are given little hints & tips about life and existence in general opposed to actually having being told directly. I think Morpheus in *The Matrix* puts it best: "Unfortunately no one can be told what the Matrix is. One must see it for themselves." I think that moment comes when we die, we are finally cleared up on what the hell is really going on behind the scenes (political secrets too I hope) in the earthly goal to discover the meaning of life. In a way we will be shown the truth, as in the Matrix.

Orbs:

A friend of mine told me once of orbs she had been photographing recently. I had heard of the concept but with all the conspiracy/alien/ghost documentaries I've seen I never saw them as 'proof.' She explained her new camera started taking pictures of them (with and without flash). They appear to be small circular energy balls; they come in various 'molds'. Some have a clear inside and others are a full circle. They tend to appear around people as if hovering next to heads/bodies/etc. Some of her pictures were taken in graveyards, some in hotel rooms, and others at parties/events. They come in different sizes due to distance from the lens and can be singular or in the majority several at once. A Facebook page has been set up where one can see some of the photos and even a video promo regarding moving footage. This evidence can only be seen with either a flash or night vision. They cannot appear to human eyes but instead in infra-red cameras they can be seen in abundance. Realists say they are flares hitting the camera lens, but I disagree. They must be real, right?

I can only summarize that they are spirits or entities, but what if they are something else? ie alien CCTV security cameras. I can only speculate, since even 'rods' can only be seen in video footage when slowed down. It is amazing to think we can capture energy simply by having infrared or night-vision mode on our cameras. If ghosts are for real than there must be some kind of afterlife. Depending on how a person dies it affects their 'souls' some are trapped on our plane and others go somewhere else; space perhaps who really knows for certain?

TRIPPING IN FILMS

Since movies are my expertise, I thought I could recommend some tripped out shit. My whole life I would make lists of various things and this is one of them. Most are famous so if haven't seen 'em - check it out:

1) *Blueberry* aka *Renegade* (2004) Dir: Jan Kounen

In my top three choices this is a terrible western film (it flopped by the way) yet has the most amazing visual depiction of tripping ever in a film. Skip to the last third of the movie and Vincent Kassel and Michael Madsen take a spiritual concoction of Mescalin made using a sacred remedy from the local Native Americans in their sacred mountain. This is more accurate to an Ayahuasca (hallucinogenic vine) trip in the South American Amazon rainforest. In the trip, Kassel's subconscious animal spirits battle it out with evil creatures from Madsen's subconscious. This CG fest is a literal translation to light (good) versus dark (evil). Despite the rest of the film this is truly one of my most important Blu-Ray/DVD's I own.

2) *Enter the Void* (2010) Dir: Gaspar Noe

My favorite tripping film of all time this tells the story of American siblings living in Tokyo, Japan. While he is reading the Tibetan Book of the Dead Oscar smokes DMT which has totally accurate visuals and sound FX for the tripping universe. Director Gaspar Noe (*Irreversible*) must have tripped before since his style in the film. He shows us the story with three different camera angles throughout to provide a journey with or without drugs.

3) *A Field in England* (2013) Dir: Ben Wheatley

I didn't enjoy this B&W experimental period film at first having liked the director's previous film *Sightseers* a lot more. I was pleasantly surprised by one of the best edited scenes in film tripping history. Very reminiscent of *Easy Rider*'s use of cuts and repeating sound FX it is a mini masterpiece/masterclass in editing alone.

4) *Beavis and Butthead Do America* (1996) Dir: Mike Judge

The scene to look out for is when the dynamic duo are out in the desert dehydrating their nuts off. Probably going to die Beavis takes a bite out of a Peyote (Mescaline) plant. A hard core bad trip for any normal average person is 'cool' for Beavis. A cartoon music video designed and performed by *White Zombie*, Rob Zombie on vocals in particular. The last portion as he comes down has the once insane landscapes roll back into place. This description is quite accurate however not as fast, even though time is distorted a trip will be a lot more stretched out.

5) *Altered States* (1980) Dir: Ken Russell

A classic film not only for revolutionary special FX, but also for William Hurt's transition through time; with the help of a potent mix of drugs (Peyote, mushies, and LSD). He is affected mentally, but physically also. At the end his wife touches him and trips as well. A must see.

6) *Fear and Loathing in Las Vegas* (1998) Dir: Terry Gilliam

Johnny Depp and Benicio del Toro bring Hunter S. Thompson's semi road-trip movie through Las Vegas to life. One of the best trippin moments is when they first arrive at the Hotel reception and Depp is already trippin.

As he sees a man on the telephone, the ground (flowery carpet) grows into the man's leg. Short, effective and very enlightening.

7) *Easy Rider* (1969) Dir: Dennis Hopper

With the production quality looking like a well-made student film, Hopper relied on no budget but with a great film outcome. "He made a film that defined the generation" many say, they were right. Whenever someone mentions 60's or 70's films, *Easy Rider* will pop up guaranteed. Choppy editing leaves stuff out, but is perfect for the trippin in the graveyard scene. One of the prozzies has a bad one, but gets naked anyway. The Mardi Gras spirit wierded out them and the viewer. The sound FX enhance the repetitious trip which can occur in real trips, brain lapses if you will. See my *bad trip* for the loops.

8) *The Doors* (1991) Dir: Oliver Stone

In his depiction of Jim Morrison, Val Kilmer's performance makes him totally believable as the rock god. Drugs did kill him, but you can see his fascination with them, especially the spiritual side at the beginning. In the desert when he trips with his band for the first time, he takes a stroll and ends up in a cave with a Native American Indian (spirit) who shows him his own death.

9) *Natural Born Killers* (1994) Dir: Oliver Stone

Again in the desert, Mickey (Woody Harrelson) and Mallory (Juliette Lewis) get paranoid when a cop tails them. In the Special Features you see how director and producer (Jane Hamsher) have a similar trip that inspired the scene. Just taken shrooms, they drive off the main road and end up lost until they find (another) Native American Indian. Together with brief cuts of rotting fruit and back projections we follow the uneasy scene. Mickey has nightmares and shoots the Holy Man, killing him in the process. Also revealing that they are demons BTW.

10) *The Bear* (1988) Dir: Jean-Jacques Annaud

A film with few humans, mainly focusing on the life of one bear cub and his adventures into adulthood. His journey begins with eating some magic mushies and having a bad trip mainly of giant frogs jumping and croaking everywhere. They look a little fake, but it's the point that counts.

11) *Training Day* (2001) Dir: Antoine Fuqua

When Denzel Washington gives Ethan Hawke a pipe to smoke telling him its weed, it's actually PCP. All part of his master plan in the story, Hawke sees everything through a colored filter (yellow-greenish) and feels like his trippin. Great visuals.

12) *Trainspotting* (1996) Dir: Danny Boyle

Director Danny Boyle and I have never taken H, I can only slightly relate to Ewan McGregor's detox/come down. His hallucinations are not only realistically disturbing, but highly relevant. The music for this scene is also perfect. Earlier, Renton OD's and literally sinks into the carpet having red carpeting on the sides of his vision. They only go away once he is injected with something from a nurse.

13) *Doberman* (1997) Dir: Jan Kounen

After his puppy dies during a robbery, the big guy is tormented. He can't take his eyes off of National Geographic on TV. When a transvestite has him sniff something, he has an instant bad trip seeing his dog in her outfit rolling over. This is editing at its finest, in this case intercut with hyena images as well.

14) *A Home at the End of the World* (2004) Dir: Michael Mayer

Before you meet Colin Farrell, we see his character as a kid trippin with his brother. Later he trips with his new best friend who experiences some visuals too.

15) *The Beach* (2000) Dir: Danny Boyle

When lonely Leo is losing the plot in the jungle he is literally becoming a soldier in his head as he sits in a canopy. He eats a caterpillar, and starts 'seeing things' one assumes it's because of his worm meal. You never know if it's really his mind or not, since it takes affect so fast. A funny video game sequence commences too.

16) *Pulp Fiction* (1994) Dir: Quentin Tarantino

After John Travolta injects himself he cruises along with rear projection (obviously fake) he smiles. Not only is his acting stoned (on H.) perfect, QT's use of backdrop purposely paying homage to his film noir heroes. Genius.

17) *Domino* (2005) Dir: Tony Scott

The bounty hunters take Mescaline and crash their truck/van in the middle of desert then a preacher appears and talks some sense into Domino (Kiera Knightley).

18) *Knocked Up* (2007) Dir: Judd Apatow

Seth Rogan and Paul Rudd go to Las Vegas to blow off some steam, so after getting lap dances from strippers they go see Circe de Solais. Seth starts havin a bad trip so they leave.

19) *Dumbo* (1941) & other Disney films Dir: Various

Having recently read the book *Elephants on Acid* by Alex Boese I was terribly shocked by the knowledge of LSD being given to animals in the 60's & 70's in the name of science. He mentions the Dumbo tripping scene, considerably one of the most tripping referenced ever in a Disney production. It literally is the beginning of the phrase "pink elephants." Everyone thinks Disney films are innocent kiddie fare, I believe there are some hidden messages and references regarding drug use (and others), this being the best example.

20) *Taking Woodstock* (2009) Dir: Ang Lee

Director Ang Lee has made two very powerful films for me: *Life of Pi* & *Crouching Tiger Hidden Dragon*. He has a very spiritual side to his film making (with some exceptions) it is briefly shown in this 70's hippie film showing another side to the Woodstock music festival. Demetri Martin takes some LSD in a camper van and colors start changing and visual movement occurs. It is very similar to the *Fear & Loathing* lobby scene and true to most hallucinations that I can confirm.

16) *Fierce People* (2005) Dir: Griffin Dunne

With Donald Sutherland and Diane Lane, as her son Finn takes some liquid acid given to him by his girlfriends' brother. Since he is into a South American tribe (because of his Dad) he lies on his bed while a Shaman prays over him and he is surrounded by rainforest. He wears a monkey skull with feathers too.

17) *Death at a Funeral* (2007) Dir: Frank Oz

When Alan Tudyk is sprightly stressed, his girlfriend gives him a valium. Little do they know that it is actually a concoction of a friend's special stash. It has Acid, Peyote, and Ketamine so you can imagine, he gets pretty fuct. He ends up naked and nearly jumping off the funeral building.

18) *A Million ways to die in the West* (2014) Dir: Seth McFarlane

Seth McFarlane's character drinks a whole gourd of Peyote and has a hippy/happy dance-musical number trip. He sees trippy colors and sheep, it ends with him kicking a giant bird in the nuts. It's basically a live action version of tripping in *Family Guy*.

19) *Amazonia* (2014) Dir: Thierry Ragobert

The main monkey eats a red mushroom and trips out to jungle audio/visuals and has flashbacks of his journey so far. The scene is intercut with the monkey drifting in and out of consciousness. Reminds me of *The Bear*.

20) *Hammer of the Gods* (2013) Dir: Farren Blackburn

Steinar arm wrestles a rival as he gets his drink laced. He sees trippy visuals intercut with his opponent still wrestling him. An interesting take on Viking history.

21) *Don Peyote* (2014) Dir: Dan Foggler & co.

Starring Dan Foggler (*Fanboys*) finally takes some Ayhuasca (not Peyote) with Josh Duhamel (*Transformers*) and has a musical trip whilst in their van and ending up in the desert. Worth a watch for the history lesson.

22) *Snow White & the Huntsman* (2013) Dir: Rupert Sanders

Starring Kristen Stewart of *Twilight* fame this is definitely the darkest version of Snow White. The scene in question is where she is lost stumbling through the evil woods and comes across dark mushrooms. These spores are the bad guys of the piece since they instantly cause bad trips. This was my favorite part in what was supposed to be a typical Hollywood adaptation of a Disney property.

23) *The Hobbit 2: Desolation of Smaug* (2013) Dir: Peter Jackson

Like *Snow White* our main characters stumble upon the 'sick woods' with a trippy vibe occurring once going off track. The only way to evade tripping is to climb up the trees and breathe fresh air. A metaphor is in there somewhere. LOL.

24) *Necessary Death of Charlie Countryman* (2013) Dir: Frederik Bond

Shia LeBeouf gets his drink laced with a combination of Ecstasy and some kind of trip, since his visuals can't come off of a pill right? He has arrived in Eastern Europe for self-discovery and briefly ends up with James Buckley from *Inbetweeners* and Rupert Grint aka Ron Weasley from the *Harry Potter* series partying in a hostel. The best bit is all the girls become naked and walk around normally as if no big deal. That trip reminds me of a UK low budget arty film and my friend China's trip in this book.

25) *ABC's of Death* Dir: Various

Two of the alphabetical horror shorts stuck out with me for obvious reasons. One, "O for Orgasm" a chick is getting choked and hallucinates trippy colors and bubbles. Second, "W for WTF" with Bad trip visuals not sure how to explain it besides hot chicks shooting laser guns some crazy giant walrus and is trippy as hell.

26) *Hot Tub Time Machine 2* Dir: Steve Pink

John Cusak's son played by Adam Scott takes drugs at a party and has a fast hectic super trip in the future, crazy colors on the dance floor scene.

27) *Electricity* Dir: Bryn Higgins

The main actress has migraines and *hallucinations* just before epileptic fits. The visuals themselves can be explained through Oliver Sacks' book Hallucinations. He describes all the various types of visual and auditory hallucinations and their reasons.

TRIPPING IN TV

1) *The Simpsons* (Ep ?) Creator: Matt Groening

In various episodes all the characters trip at one point. Shrooms and LSD secretly find their way into food or drink. Watch out for their eyes you'll know when.

2) *South Park* (Ep?) Creator(s): Trey Parker, Matt Stone

Mr. Mackey lectures that 'drugs are bad, um kay' then ends up doing every type of drug (booze/weed/LSD). His head turns into a balloon, just like me in my *bad trip*.

3) *X-Files* (Ep?) Creator: Chris Carter

This taboo episode was far from the usual alien conspiracies, this time with an hallucinogenic cave. Hallucinating in his head (in this case Mulder) he lives out various situations. 'Stuck' in one sense of the word refers to being physically comatose but mentally active, which ends up with Skully finding Mulder still trippin covered in slime. His trip ending with the assassination of his boss Skinner.

3) *Family Guy* (Episode "Let's go to the Hop") Creator: Seth Macfarlane

Originally I didn't really like this show, I felt the animation was too clunky. But then I started getting the humor and appreciating all the homage's to films. This episode dealt with the Colombian tripping toad, where u like it and get visuals. The rest deals with Peter (the Dad) going undercover to stop the 'drug problem.' Another episode worth watching is when Brian is killed off he is running around Hell with many trippy incarnations of the Family members.

4) *Duckman* (Not so Easy Riders Episode) Creator: ?

Also poor animation (2-D), but with innuendos only grown-ups would understand. This Easy Riders rip-off sees Duckman & Cornfed becoming Peter Fonda & Denis Hopper to avoid the IRS. They come across an Indian in the desert who gives Duckman some Chilli Tartare which makes him trip out. He sees some hippies, with the scene reminding me of Beavis & Butthead film trippin' scene.

6) House (Hallucinating Girl & House)

One episode in Season 2 has a patient hallucinating due to her medical condition; she sees House's (Hugh Laurie) skin melt off his face. In another episode we see House hallucinating in his mind leaving him and the viewers confused about what was real and what not. In Season 3 a boy is brought in believing he has been abducted by aliens, due to a condition his hallucinations appear real, but are only a distortion of reality.

7) *Entourage* (SE5 EP5 "Tree Trippers") Dir: Julian Farino Creator: Doug Ellin

Our groups of guys go out to Joshua Tree (U2 album cover) to trip so Vincent Chase can have questions answers about his future. No visuals but funny acting from the boys. Great cameo from Eric Roberts too.

8) 4400 (SE3 EP7 "Blink") Dir: Colin Bucksey

In this episode of the supernatural show the town suffers from hallucinations of dead family members. Is it a virus from the alien race, the future or side effects from something else. It reminded me of the X-Files episode mentioned above.

Trippy Films - Recommended viewing

1) *The Matrix* (1999) Dir(s): Wachowski Bros (errrr siblings)

The bit to skip to is when Neo (Keanu Reeves) takes the red pill and is about to tumble down the rabbit hole. He sits in a chair and notices the mirror next to him as he touches it and pulls away a silver liquid (like T-1000) attached to his arm, it continues to enter his mouth. He is then transported, with an eerie sound into the future (real world). In Part 3 (*Revolutions*): Blind Neo sees light everywhere.

2) *Pink Floyd: The Wall* (1982) Dir: Alan Parker

One long music video with live-action and cartoons it is ideal to watch stoned or inebriated. Semi plot relies on visuals to carry the film.

3) *The Yellow Submarine* (1968) Dir: George Dunning

For kids and adults it is very kitsch, but for trippers we notice the beginning when you are first introduced to the characters. Their houses/rooms move around in a weird choreography.

4) *The Cell* (2000) Dir: Tarsem Singh

Visually one of the best films ever, relying on a gripping story and amazing CG moments. The music video style adds to the dimensions of Jenifer Lopez' trips into the serial killer's (Vincent D'Onofrio) mind. Each trip becomes more intense and trippy. When Vince Vaughn's character is sent in to save J-Lo his first time he experiences full-on hallucinations.

5) *Wizard of Oz* (1939) Dir(s): Various

Seeing the tornado for the first time is ahead of its time FX. Along with a transition of B&W to color is fantastic. Watching the sets and production design alone is enough.

6) *Heavenly Creatures* (1994) Dir: Peter Jackson

This true story focuses on two New Zealand girls murder of one of their mothers. The journey into insanity is when they create their own fairytale world in their heads. The best bit when they first are both transported to that world with large butterflies, soldiers, and rainbows. Along with CG bringing their world to life, Kate Winslet's shines in her breakthrough performance.

7) *Lawnmower Man* (1992) Dir: Brett Leonard

Jeff Fahey plays a mentally disabled lawn mower, who is given the chance to increase his IQ with virtual reality video games. Pierce Brosnan pushes the boundaries of Jobe's mind when he starts to have terrible headaches. But in return he gets to play God in virtual reality world. With altered brain waves his only goal is to conquer the world.

8) *My Life* (1993) Dir: Bruce Joel Rubin

After Michael Keaton discovers he has cancer he goes to a Chinese chiropractor who massages him, he blacks out and sees trippy visuals. Just the one scene unfortunately.

9) *Holy Smoke* (1999) Dir: Jane Campion

Leading onto a similar moment when Kate Winslet's character is singled out by a guru and touched on the forehead, she falls back hallucinating big time. It changes her whole view on life and Harvey Keitel is brought in to cure her, ending up nuts himself.

10) *Virtuosity* (1995) Dir: Brett Leonard

When plugged in Denzel Washington is in a virtual reality world controlled by Russell Crowe. Parts of the CG are meant to look artificial, but similar to a videogame. All the mods have their programs.

11) *007: James Bond* (Opening title sequences) Dir: Various

All the Bonds have got great openings, but the title sequences are done extremely well too. Along with title songs performed by stars they are highly watchable. In particular see *World is Not Enough* it's definitely supposed to be 60's/70's colors with bright trippy imagery. Twisting and twirling background layers usually in silhouette and melting women in the foreground. In this case the title song is performed by Garbage.

12) *Secretary* (2002) Dir: Steven Shainberg

A fuct-up tale of a messed up girl (Maggie Gyllenthal) who falls in love with her boss (James Spader). At one point she is fantasizing about her boyfriend then her boss, she starts masturbating in bed and is transported. She imagines him sitting there (w/ colorful lighting) watching her. It's as if she's so ecstatic she hallucinates just from touching herself. Women - god bless 'em.

13) *Alexander* (2005) Dir: Oliver Stone

Alexander the Great is played by Colin Farrell, this time you see him looking at his Mom (Angelina Jolie) in his cup of wine, before he drinks it. She has medusa's head warning him of typhoid, he gulps it down anyway. Some say he predicted his own death at a young age, others just considered him an "alki" (alcoholic).

14) *Constantine* (2005) Dir: Francis Lawrence

Whenever Keanu Reeves "steps-over" into Hell he is in an identical world to ours just Hellish trippy. Sound is also key with the visuals. Both this and another of the director's other films *I Am Legend* are visual masterpieces to me.

15) *Animatrix* (Matriculated 2003) Dir: Peter Chung

My personal favorite of the shorts. When the converting robot is inside the humans matrix converting program he is subjected to various trippy sequences especially when he's with the 'matrix humans'. Can robots trip is the same as asking if animals can trip: of course.

16) *A Beautiful Mind* (2001) Dir: Ron Howard

Director Ron Howard's best film to date in my opinion, not only emotional and thrilling but exquisite performances too. Russell Crowe plays real-life schizo Professor John Nash. Unable to tell the difference between imaginary friends/colleagues his hallucinations can only be stopped through medication, if he takes them. There are many moments in the film worthwhile mentioning, but one in particular is when he makes an acquaintance with a fellow student and his tie. Light refractions are seen and glowing lines appear from a glass of water matching with the tie.

17) *Interview with a Vampire* (1994) Dir: Neil Jordan

When Brad Pitt first becomes one of the undead his new powers excite him. He looks around and sees moving statues and light alternates in his vision.

18) All *Predators* (1987/1990/2004/2007) Dir: Various

Whenever you see the Predator's vision it reminds you of a cooler version of thermal (night-vision) goggles. You see he is connected electrically to his helmet. It's a shame you never get to see B&W Aliens vision, from the AVP games.

19) *LOTR* trilogy (2000-2003) Dir: Peter Jackson

Every time Frodo puts on the "ring of power" he is invisible yet in Sauron's vision. Starting off farther away zooming in, wind blowing all over the place. Towards the end of the films he literally sees Sauron's eye as a searchlight.

20) *Harry Potter* (all) Dir: Various

The magic (i.e. CG) is cool not just for kids, but adults alike. In part 3 (*Prisoner of Azkaban*): The use of the timepiece to rewind time, shown in one shot literally.

21) DP Vittorio Storarro films (*Apocalypse Now/Exorcist Prequel/Godfather trilogy*)

Using lights on a dimmer switch for *Apocalypse Now*, his exposure was remote controlled. He managed to create the moodiest atmospheres besides DP Bob Richardson (Oliver Stone & Quentin Tarantino) films. Not necessarily always working on the best of films, but I consider him one of the top DP's of all time.

22) *Zeitgesit(s)* Dir: ?

This enlightening trippy documentary exposes all conspiracies revolving around 9/11, Income Tax, similarities between Hitler and Bush, etc. Trippy edits/transitions make the film(s) highly educational.

23) *2001* (1968) Dir: Stanley Kubrick

Saving the best for last. Flopping at first then becoming a cult classic (like most of Kubrick's films). This sci-fi epic space journey goes beyond science and into deep spiritualism. Even I totally misunderstood it at first but after several viewings and reading about it I finally get what he was trying to say. Not only was this film nearly a decade before the Star Wars revolution, Kubrick was a genius regardless ahead of everybody else film-wise. The ending is one of the most famous "mind-fuck" moments in cinema's history.

ACKNOWLEDGEMENTS

Firstly I would like to thank Gaia or mother earth (Rangi) since she and heavenly father (Papa) have created this realm. Some call it God others 'mother earth' it all boils down to the same beliefs really. Life is a miracle regardless; some say the key to existence is found in Pi (Pythagoras). It can be found in the Fibonacci sequence also known as mathematical fractals. They can be found in all forms of life: plants, cells, DNA. I thank science for explaining many mysteries and still providing more and more insights into our lives daily. I appreciate my parents for creating me and friends and family that have helped form me. My English (father's) side provided me with insights into the Christian/Catholic world giving me a base of remaining a good person to this day. My German (mother's) side gave me the introduction to a cooler way of life including great food and drink and even my some of my first drug experiences too. My brother has been a companion for those drug fueled days when I was searching for 'answers' and he was searching for 'highs.' Will Slepton for editing my book being the first person to read the whole piece and see an insight into my life so far. Cats have always been in my life, since they are a constant companion to the animal universe. And all the others that have helped this book become a reality.

Lasco Atkins/Mabuk Films 2009-15